fRiENd or fOE

the misadventures of Willie Plummet

PAUL BUCHANAN
& ROD RANDALL

CPH
SAINT LOUIS

The Misadventures of Willie Plummet

Cover illustration by John Ward.
Back cover photo by Ira Lippke.
Cover and interior design by Karol Bergdolt.

Scripture quotations are taken from the HOLY BIBLE, NEW INTERNATIONAL VERSION. NIV®. Copyright ©1973, 1978, 1984 by International Bible Society. Used by permission of Zondervan Publishing House. All rights reserved.

Copyright © 1999 Paul Buchanan
Published by Concordia Publishing House
3558 S. Jefferson Avenue, St. Louis, MO 63118-3968
Manufactured in the United States of America

Library of Congress Cataloging-in-Publication Data

Buchanan, Paul, 1959-
   Friend or foe / Paul Buchanan and Rod Randall.
      p. cm. — (The misadventures of Willie Plummet ; 16)
   Summary: Hoping to win an award so his high school will receive grant money for computers, Willie takes on a series of disastrous volunteer activities while at the same time caught up in a conflict with his best friend.
    ISBN 0-570-07005-8
   [1. Best friends—Fiction. 2. Voluntarism—Fiction. 3. High schools—Fiction.
4. Schools—Fiction.] I. Randall, Rod, 1962- . II. Title.
PZ7.B87717Fr 2000
[Fic]—dc21
                              99-046867

1 2 3 4 5 6 7 8 9 10   08 07 06 05 04 03 02 01 00 99

For Vincent

Contents

1

My Work with the League of Women Voters Finally Pays Off

It was five minutes before the first bell rang at Glenfield Middle School. I was pulling my science book out of my locker when Felix, one of my two best friends, came up behind me.

"I've been looking all over for you, Dude," Felix told me.

"Call off the search," I told him. "I'm right here."

Felix didn't smile. He pushed his glasses higher on his nose. "I've got some bad news," Felix said, not looking me in the eye. "I'm not going to be able to work on our History of the West project this weekend."

"What?" I said. "Our projects are due in three weeks. You promised we'd work on them together. Butch Cassidy and the Sundance Kid—the buddies of the Old West. You can't do this to me." I slammed my locker door and twisted the combination lock.

"Dude, I don't like it any more than you," Felix told me. "But there's nothing I can do. My folks are going out of town for a few weeks. They're shipping me off to my aunt's house in Pepperville."

"What about school?" I asked him.

"My aunt's going to drop me off every morning and pick me up right after school lets out," Felix told me. "I won't even be able to come into town on the weekends. Believe me; I'm sick about it."

"You're 13," I said. "You're responsible. Won't your parents let you stay on your own?"

"Don't you think I already tried that?" Felix said. "It was a no go."

"Why?" I asked. "Don't your parents trust you?" Felix didn't seem to want to talk about it. "Come on, Felix," I pushed him. "If you're going to ruin my grade in history, at least you can tell me the whole story."

Felix groaned and looked down the hallway. "They said they trusted *me* enough—it was someone else they had a problem with," he said.

"What are you talking about?"

"*You*, Willie," Felix said. "It's *you* they were worried about."

"*Me*?"

"Well, no offense, Dude," Felix said. "But even with adult supervision you're pretty dangerous. They were worried you might come over and blow up our house."

"I've never blown up a house," I objected. It was the truth. I'd blown up a number of other things—but never a house. "This is so typical!" I said. "A few innocent explosions and people brand you for life! A couple of the explosions weren't even my fault."

Felix just looked down at the floor and shook his head. "Face it, Dude," he said. "You're a one-man wrecking crew. And my parents *like* our house."

I sighed and headed down the hall toward the stairs. Felix fell in beside me. "Well, how about if we *have* some adult supervision?" I asked. "Would they let you stay in town then?"

"I don't know," he said. "What do you have in mind?" We started down the stairs.

"What if you moved in with me for a couple of weeks?" I asked. "My house is crawling with adults. We could share my room. We wouldn't have to go near your precious house."

Felix shrugged again. "I guess it's worth a try," he said. "You ask your folks and I'll ask mine."

For some reason I wanted Felix to be a bit more enthusiastic about the prospect of becoming my roommate. "Worth a *try*?" I said. "Felix, we'd have the time of our lives. Two best friends, sharing a room— we'll be like Butch and Sundance."

Felix didn't say anything. He looked down at his wristwatch just as the first bell rang. "If you say so," he said. Felix turned and headed down the hall toward his first class.

"Like Butch and Sundance," I called after him. "You'll see." I turned and headed in the opposite direction toward Mr. Keefer's class.

I came in the room just as the second bell rang. Mr. Keefer was still ransacking his desk for his blue roll book. He was a good guy, but he was a bit absent-minded. I sat down at a desk in the back that Sam had saved for me. Sam, whose real name is Samantha, is my other best friend.

Sam tucked her blond hair behind her ears and leaned closer to me. "Did Felix give you the bad news?" she asked.

"Yeah," I told her. "But I think we've got it worked out so he can stay in town."

Sam smiled and nodded. "Cool."

Mr. Keefer must have heard my voice. "Willie," he said from the front of the room. "You're just the one I wanted to see. Could I have a word with you before class starts?" He motioned for me to come to the front of the class. I glanced over at Sam and got up from my desk.

Maybe it's just me, but when a teacher wants to talk to me, I always assume the worst. On my way to the front, I tried to think of what I'd done to get in trouble. I lead a pretty active life, so by the time I got to the front row, I'd already thought of a dozen things I might get yelled at for.

Mr. Keefer smiled at me. He stroked his beard and glanced around like he didn't want others to hear. "Willie, I really appreciate all you did to help organize the Science Fair Fund-raiser last week," he told me. "I'm very impressed with your community spirit."

"Thank you, sir," I said, instantly relieved that I wasn't going to get yelled at.

"And I know how hard you worked heading up the canned food drive last month," Mr. Keefer went on.

I could have told him that it was really Missy Urrutia who had headed up the food drive, but with Mr. Keefer it can be difficult to correct a mistaken impression, so I just nodded.

"And I know how involved you are with hospital visitation, the Big Brother program, and the Scholarship Society," he continued.

Jessica Lenahan, Ryan Hardy, and Patrick Garcia, I could have told him, but I didn't. We'd all given up long ago on ever straightening out Mr. Keefer's confusion.

"Anyway, I'm very impressed with your involvement," he told me. "So at our last faculty meeting, I insisted that you be our school's official nominee for the Van Andel Citizenship Award."

I smiled and nodded. He didn't have a clue, but I knew I should be polite. "Thank you, sir," I told him. "Thank you very much."

Mr. Keefer handed me a slightly crumpled leaflet. "This is your part of the application," he said. "Make sure you fill it out in detail and turn it in on time. It could mean a lot to our school."

I looked down at the wrinkled paper in my hand. I had no idea what he was talking about. "Sure thing, Mr. Keefer," I said. "I'll get right on it."

Sam stared at me curiously as I made my way back to her, the application form in my hands. "What was that all about?" she asked as I took my seat.

"Oh, he nominated me for some citizenship award," I told her. "He seems to think I invented the polio vaccine and head up the local chapter of the League of Women Voters. It's nothing. I'm just glad I'm not in trouble."

"He didn't nominate you for the Van Andel Award, did he?" Sam asked.

"Something like that," I said. "He's so confused he might have nominated me for Homecoming Queen."

"This is serious, Willie," Sam said. "Haven't you ever heard of the Van Andel Award?"

I shrugged. "What is it, some kind of trophy?"

Sam shook her head. "It's a big grant," she told me. "Thousands of dollars for computers and software. They award it to one school in our district every year."

I stared at her blinking. "You're pulling my leg."

"No," she told me. "They started giving it out a couple of years ago. That's how Central High got all that high-tech equipment in their library."

"No way," I said. "Do you know how much equipment like that costs?"

"Do you know how rich Stephen Van Andel is?" Sam asked me back. "He invented some kind of marketing software. He's got hundreds of millions of dollars."

"Yeah, right," I said. "Like anyone with that kind of money would live here in Glenfield. If he was that rich, he'd live in New York or Paris or someplace cool."

"You don't get it," Sam said. "He lives all over the place. But he's got a house here in town because he grew up here. His mother still lives here."

I flattened the application out on my desk. Sure enough, it was an application for the Van Andel Citizenship Award. At the top, Mr. Keefer had filled in my name. Beneath that was a bunch of space to fill in my community service activities. I flipped through the pages. There was space to write an essay and a bunch of other things to fill out.

"And this guy goes around giving money to schools?" I was still a little doubtful. "What's his angle?"

Sam rolled her eyes. "There's no *angle*," she said. "It's called giving back to the community. He wants to encourage community-minded students." She grinned. "How in the world did *you* get nominated?"

Sam was right. I hadn't done nearly as much community service as some other students I knew. "Remember the work I did at the Science Fair Fundraiser?" I asked. "That's why I got nominated."

Sam leaned closer. "You only volunteered to clean up at the fund-raiser so you could get the leftover chemicals and equipment," she reminded me.

"Yeah," I said. I looked down at the application form. "Maybe I can put down that I'm active in recycling."

Sam rolled her eyes. "Willie," she said. "This award is supposed to go to someone dedicated to helping others—someone who works hard to make this community a better place."

I rubbed the back of my neck. "I brought thousands of dollars worth of business to this town with my Skyrunner 1000," I told her.

"I don't think starting a UFO scare counts as community service," Sam said.

I glanced up at Mr. Keefer. He was still looking for his roll book. My school could really use the computer equipment, but Mr. Keefer had definitely nominated the wrong student. I looked down at the application. The deadline to turn it in was three weeks away. "I've got three weeks," I whispered to Sam. "I can do a lot of volunteer work in three weeks."

②

On the Trail of Butch Cassidy

When the final bell rang, I headed downstairs to the school library. I needed some books for my History of the West project.

I went to the card catalogue and looked up "Cassidy, Butch." I found three titles. I wrote the call numbers in my notebook and went to look for them.

When I found the shelf where the books should have been, none of them were there. Why would anyone check them all out? I was the only kid in the school doing his report on Butch Cassidy. Felix signed us up for Butch and Sundance weeks ago.

I went out to the flagpole, where I usually meet Sam and Felix after school. Sam was waiting patiently for Felix and me to show up.

"I can't walk home with you guys today," I told her while the flag flapped noisily overhead. "I've got to go to the public library. You going to wait for Felix?"

"I'll give him a few more minutes," she said.

"Do me a favor," I said to Sam. "Tell him to make sure he asks his parents about moving in with me. I'll call him tonight after dinner."

"I'll give him your message," Sam said. "Why are you going to the library?"

"I need to get some books for my History of the West project," I told her. "Some Butch Cassidy fanatic checked out all the books in our library. Who did you pick for your project?"

"Annie Oakley, of course," she said. "She was the best shot in the West—even though everyone told her girls couldn't shoot."

I grinned. "That's a pretty fitting choice," I told her. Sam was always trying to prove that a girl could do pretty much anything a boy could. "You going to shoot a piece of chalk out of Mrs. Vaughan's mouth when you do your presentation?"

Sam smiled. "As long as I can practice on you," she told me. "Who's Felix doing his project on?"

"The Sundance Kid," I told her. "Butch Cassidy and the Sundance Kid—the Wild West's Best Buddies."

"Another fitting choice," Sam said.

When I got to the library, I found an open computer and typed in "Cassidy, Butch." This time I got five titles. I wrote the numbers on a scrap of paper.

I found the correct aisle and moved along it, trying to find the call numbers I'd written down. One other kid was in the same aisle, sitting on the floor, bent over a book. He had short brown hair and a baseball cap turned backwards. I recognized him from church—he was in the high school group with my brother, Orville. His name was TJ Drew.

I passed behind him and found the correct call numbers at the far end of the row. The books I needed were on the top shelf. I stood on my tiptoes and stretched. They were just out of reach.

I considered climbing up on the bottom shelf so I could reach the books—but knowing me, the whole shelf would topple over, sending a domino chain reaction throughout the entire library. I sighed. Felix's parents weren't exaggerating much; disasters *do* tend to happen when I'm around. I looked down the aisle.

"Hey, TJ," I whispered. "I need some books on the top shelf. Do you think you could get them down for me?"

TJ looked over and smiled. He seemed to be a pretty cool guy. "No problem," he said. He put his open book face down on the carpet and stood up. "You're Orville's brother, aren't you?" he said, coming down the aisle toward me.

"A lot of people make that mistake," I said. "Actually he's *my* brother."

TJ smiled.

"My name's Willie," I told him, holding out my hand. "Wilbur, actually. Orville and Wilbur. Pathetic, huh?"

TJ grinned and shook my hand. "TJ Drew," he said. "It stands for Thomas Jefferson. That's *almost* as pathetic." TJ looked up at the shelf. "Which books?" he asked.

"Those ones up there." I pointed.

Without even raising to his tiptoes, TJ pulled the books out one by one and passed them down to me.

"Cool," I said. "Thanks."

A few minutes later, I was in the checkout line with my five Butch Cassidy books. Some lady up at the front of the line was arguing with the librarian about a fine, so the line didn't move for a few minutes.

To pass the time, I read the flyers tacked to the bulletin board. One advertised a science fiction reading group. Another was about an adult literacy program. Then I noticed one that said Teen Volunteers across the top.

It occurred to me that this was a chance to do something I could put on my Van Andel Award nomination form. I could come out to the library some afternoon, shelve some books, and earn the right to call myself a library volunteer. How hard could working in a library be? All you really need to know is the alphabet, and I knew it backwards and forwards. Well, forwards anyway.

When I got to the front of the line, I put my books on the counter. "Sorry you had to wait so long," the librarian said. She had long, braided black hair. She opened the books and stacked them one on top of the other.

"No problem," I told her. "I have plenty of time. In fact, I noticed your flyer about teen volunteers. Is there anything I could do tomorrow after school?"

The librarian stopped what she was doing and looked up at me. "Well, actually, tomorrow will be a very busy day for us," she told me. "We could really use the help. Maybe you could run the Story Hour."

I remembered the Story Hour from when I was little—all the kids sat in a circle, and some grown-up read them a picture book. It was really more like the Story Fifteen Minutes, which suited me fine. "I'd love to do the Story Hour," I told her. "When should I get here?"

I left the library and walked down to the corner feeling good, even though I still had the long walk home ahead of me. The sun was shining. Birds were singing. I'd found some good books on Butch Cassidy and my first volunteer job.

I stood at the curb whistling, waiting to cross the street, when a green pickup truck pulled up beside me. The driver leaned over and rolled down the window. It was TJ Drew.

"Want a ride home?" he asked.

I grinned. This was my day. "Sure thing," I told him.

"So what did they say?" I asked Felix. "Are we going to be roommates or what?" I was talking on the kitchen cordless phone, sitting on the counter. The kitchen still smelled of the chicken we'd had for dinner.

"They said it was okay as long as your parents are home and you stay away from our house," Felix said. He paused. "Except I don't think I was supposed to tell you that last part."

I rolled my eyes. "Don't worry," I said. "We don't have to go anywhere *near* your precious house. You'll have everything you need right here."

There was a few seconds pause in the conversation. It still kind of bugged me that Felix wasn't more excited about being roommates. The refrigerator heaved and buzzed. "This will be great," I told Felix. I imagined us up in my room planning pranks and horsing around—having a great time together. "Like Butch and Sundance," I said.

I heard a click on the phone, like someone had picked up the extension. I heard Orville groan and put the phone down again. Orville had been in a foul mood for more than a week since his girlfriend had dumped him. He insisted she dumped him because he brought her over to dinner once and I told her all about the Ninja Turtle underwear he used to wear—but of course that wasn't the real reason.

"Okay," Felix said. "I guess I should go and start packing. Mom said she could drop me off Saturday morning."

"Excellent," I said. "I'll get my room ready. We've got a folding cot you can sleep on. It's very comfortable."

Orville came storming through the swinging kitchen door. "Get off the phone you little dork," he said. "I've got to make a call."

"I'll be done in a minute," I told him.

Orville just stood there glaring at me. I took the phone away from my ear and covered the mouthpiece with my hand. "Do you mind?" I said. "It'll only take *one* minute."

Orville didn't budge.

I rolled my eyes. "Look, why don't you go in the living room, find a scrap of paper, and write down everything you know. That should take about a minute."

Orville didn't move a muscle. He just stood glaring at me. I put the phone to my ear. I didn't really have anything else to say to Felix—I was just about to say good-bye when Orville came in—but I hated to have him think I was getting off the phone on his account. I just sat there on the counter a few seconds with the phone to my ear, not saying anything.

"Dude," Felix said on the other end of the phone. "You still there?"

I paused a few more seconds, trying to look unhurried. "I'll see you tomorrow, Felix," I said into the phone. "I'm glad this worked out. We're going to have a great time."

When Felix said good-bye, I pushed the hang-up button on the cordless phone and held it out to Orville. He huffed and snatched it from my hand. He dialed his number, ignoring me completely.

In a way I felt sorry for him. His girlfriend had dumped him, and in a couple of days, when Felix moved in, he'd be outnumbered. Felix and I would rule this house.

I hopped down off the counter and pushed through the swinging kitchen door.

③

Cutthroat Sally Sinks the Spanish Armada

I arrived at the library about 15 minutes before the children's Story Hour was supposed to begin. The parking lot was full, and cars were parked along the curb a block or two in every direction. Traffic was terrible. A lot of men and women in suits stood around outside the front entrance. And a news van, its engine running, was parked illegally at a red curb. What was going on here?

Inside, the library was packed—more crowded than I'd ever seen it. People were milling around everywhere. There were lots more men and women in suits. They looked like people who should be at work right now. The library staff at the desk seemed frazzled and distracted by all the commotion. The librarian I'd spoken to yesterday was talking urgently on the phone. She looked stressed. She kept twisting her long, black braid in her fingers.

I headed back to the children's section. I thought I'd get things ready and give the librarian a chance to finish her phone call. The children's section was a lot smaller than I remembered it. Tiny chairs were arranged around miniature tables, and there were picture books strewn everywhere. There were only four or five children in the section, pawing through picture books or sitting cross-legged on the floor, pulling book after book from the shelf to see the covers.

I found a chair that was bigger than the others. I put that one in the corner and arranged some of the smaller chairs in a circle around it. That's how the Story Hour was set up when I was a kid.

When I was done, I looked over at the circulation desk. The librarian with the braid was still on the phone, so I tidied up a bit. I thought I might as well help out a little, since I was supposed to be a volunteer. I picked up some stray books and straightened up the tables and chairs. I figured I'd be out of there in 20 minutes. And then I'd go home and write "Glenfield Public Library Volunteer" on the Van Andel Award application form.

Maybe if I managed to win the award, my school library could get rid of their old card catalogues and switch to computers. Maybe there'd be enough money to put computers in all the classrooms. I had to win this award. Glenfield Middle School was behind the times; maybe this would be our chance to catch up.

The next time I glanced up at the circulation desk, the librarian was no longer on the phone; she was now scribbling something on a clipboard. I went up to the counter.

"May I help you?" the librarian asked me. She seemed pretty stressed out.

"Yes, ma'am," I said. "I'm the guy who volunteered to read a story to the kids today. Is there a book I'm supposed to read, or do I just pick one off the shelf?"

She seemed to recognize me suddenly and smiled. "Sorry," she said. "I forgot. Things are pretty frantic today. I really appreciate your willingness to pitch in. Pick any book you want. We have some excellent picture books back in the children's section."

I was hoping she'd have a book picked out for me. There were *thousands* of books in the children's section; I had no idea where to begin looking.

A flash went off behind me. I turned to see two men and a woman, all in suits, standing in front of a photographer.

I looked back at the librarian. "Is there a book you can recommend?" I asked her.

"Well, one of my favorites is *Deep in the Woods*," she said. "It was just returned. Would you like me to go back and find it for you?"

"Sure," I said. "That would be great, if it isn't too much trouble."

The librarian disappeared through the open doorway behind the counter. I turned and leaned back on the counter. I watched another group of people in suits pose for another photo. What were all these people doing taking pictures in a library? They must be the world's lamest tourists, I thought.

"Here we are," the librarian sang out cheerfully. "*Deep in the Woods.*"

I turned back to her. She set the book down on the counter in front of me. On the cover was a picture of a dark tangled forest with some kind of castle rising above the trees. There was a single light in one of the castle's towers and a full moon high in the sky. The book looked spooky and mysterious. The kids would really love this one!

"Cool," I said. Another camera flashed. I glanced over at the people in suits and back at the librarian. "What are all these people doing here?" I asked her.

"Oh, they're here because of the new wing," she said.

"New wing?"

"A new wing of the library," she said. "It hasn't been built yet. The groundbreaking is today. That's what all this fuss is about. It will be quite an addition to our little library."

"Cool," I said. "What will the new wing be for?"

"The Van Andel Wing will be full of new high-tech computer equipment," she said. "It will be a big step forward for us."

"The Van Andel Wing?" I said. "You mean like Stephen Van Andel?"

"Yes," she said. "He donated the money for the new wing. He should be here any minute for the ceremony."

I stood a moment blinking. I leaned across the counter. "Mr. Van Andel will be *here*?" I said.

"He's due any minute for the ceremony," the librarian said.

My mind heaved into overdrive. This was the perfect opportunity. If Mr. Van Andel saw me working hard as a volunteer—if he saw me reading to a bunch of thoroughly enchanted children—maybe he'd remember me when it was time to choose a winner of the Van Andel Award. *Cha-ching*!

I grabbed the book and dashed over to the children's section. I took a quick count to see how many kids there were. Six—five boys and one girl scattered throughout the children's section. That would be a decent audience, provided they all really got into it. I set the *Deep in the Woods* on the biggest chair in my reading circle and went to round up the kids.

A little boy with red hair sat at one of the tiny round tables, looking at a picture book. His elbows were on the table, and his head was propped in his hands. He was a cute little guy. He looked just like me when I was 4 or 5 years old. I went over and knelt down beside him.

"Hey," I said. "I'm going to read a cool book for Story Hour. Want to come listen?"

The boy looked up from his book. He gave me the once over. "No thanks, mister," he said. "I'm already reading a book." He propped his head on his hands again. I thought kids loved being read to, but this one was definitely unimpressed with Story Hour.

I looked out at the bustling main library. Mr. Van Andel could be here any minute. He could be on his way up the front steps right now.

"Look, kid," I said. "This is kind of important. I'll give you a dollar if you come listen and pretend like you're having a good time."

The boy looked up from the book again. He wasn't sure what to think of me. I pulled out my wallet and opened it. I pulled out a dollar bill and held it in front of his face.

The boy closed the book he was reading. "Go over and sit on one of those chairs," I told him, handing him the dollar. "And remember our deal: You have to act like you're having a good time."

The kid walked over to the circle of chairs, holding the dollar in front of him like he was reading a book. "Hey, kid," I hissed. "Put that in your pocket until after we're done, okay?" He folded the dollar and slipped it into his pocket before he sat down.

Slyly, I went from kid to kid, whispering. Four dollars later, all five boys were sitting in a semicircle around my empty chair, restlessly waiting for Story Hour to begin.

The last kid—the girl—lay on the carpet with a book open in front of her. She had curly brown hair and wore pink tights and a pink sweater. I went and stood over her. She turned her head and looked up at me with one eyebrow raised.

"I'm going to read a really cool story over there," I told her. I gestured toward the four fidgeting boys in the corner. "All those kids want to hear it. Why don't you come listen too?"

The little girl sat up and closed her book. "Only if you pay me a dollar like everyone else," she said. I guess I hadn't been as sly as I'd thought.

I sighed and pulled out my wallet. I opened it and looked inside. "I can't pay you a dollar," I told her. "All I've got left is a $5 bill."

"That'll do," she said.

I stood looking down at her. "You want me to pay you five bucks just to listen to a story?" I sputtered. "Are you crazy?"

"I can act real good," she said. "I can pretend you're the best story reader in the world." She shook her curls and gave me an enchanted smile—I suppose to show me how she would look while I was reading the story.

I sighed. For all I knew, Mr. Van Andel was in the library right now. I looked in my wallet. What was $5 worth, next to a bunch of cutting-edge computer equipment? I pulled the $5 bill out of my wallet and handed it to the girl. "For five bucks, you better act like Meryl Streep," I told her.

When my little actress finally took her seat, I picked up the book and sat down in the big chair in the corner. I looked over toward the main library. A couple of men in suits were watching us, smiling. With any luck, one of them would be Mr. Van Andel.

I opened *Deep in the Woods*. The first picture showed a princess all dressed in pink sitting in some kind of throne room. Uh-oh. I flipped through the book. There were all kinds of pink, girlish pictures— there was even one of the princess kissing some handsome prince. I looked up at my audience. I groaned. Five boys, and I'm supposed to read a *princess* story?

I glanced up. The two men in suits were still watching. I looked at the circle of children. Some of the boys were already beginning to fidget. I propped the book on my knees, opened to the first page.

"This is the story of a woman pirate," I pretended to read. "Her name was Cutthroat Sally. She always wore pink because it tricked her victims into thinking she was nice when really she was mean and treacher-ous." I turned the book around and held it up so they could see the picture.

"Hey," the little girl said. "That's not how it goes."

I'd paid her $5 to act like she was enjoying the story, and she was already heckling me. "How do *you* know what it says?" I whispered hotly. "You don't even know how to read."

"I have this book at home," she told me. "And that's *not* how it goes."

I groaned and rolled my eyes. "Well this is how it goes *today*," I told her. I held the book up so no one in the main library could see my face and gave her my most menacing look. "For five bucks I don't want to hear any complaints," I told her.

One of the boys perked up suddenly. "You gave her $5?" he said. "How come *she* gets $5?"

"Look, do you mind?" I said, still hiding my face behind the book. "I thought we all had an agreement."

I put the book back on my knees and flipped to the next page. It showed a picture of the princess running through the woods at night, looking scared. A yellow moon lit up the sky.

"Every full moon, Cutthroat Sally would go into the dark woods," I said, making it up as I went along. "Where she had trained an army of wolves and vampire bats that did her evil bidding." I held the book up so they could all see the picture.

"That's *not* how it goes," the little girl said.

I glared at her from behind the book. She was really ticking me off. "Look," I said. "The next complaint out of you will cost you a dollar."

"Yeah, but how come *she* gets $5?" one of the other boys asked. I ignored him.

I put the book back on my knees and turned to the next page. I looked down at the illustration and thought a moment. "Cutthroat Sally, the pirate who dressed in pink, loved to rob and plunder other ships," I pretended to read. "And she had these trained sharks that would tell her when a ship full of gold was coming her way."

"This is *really* a story about a princess," the little girl told the boy next to her.

I snatched the book from my knees and held it in front of my face. "That just cost you a dollar," I hissed from behind the book.

"Can I have *her* dollar?" the boy next to her wanted to know.

It took a while, but I made it through the book. When I was done, I closed it and set it on my knees. I looked down at the spooky picture on the front and shook my head. Now I knew what they meant about not judging a book by its cover!

But I had managed to make the best of it. By the end of Story Hour, Cutthroat Sally had sunk the entire Spanish fleet, captured the Hawaiian Islands, and invented the guillotine.

When the kids all scattered, I put the chairs back in place and trudged up to the circulation desk with the book under my arm, exhausted and $10 poorer. This volunteer work wasn't as easy as it looked.

The librarian was busy checking out some books for a woman. Things were much quieter in the library now. Most of the people in suits had gone outside for the groundbreaking. I wondered if Mr. Van Andel had noticed me.

A man with a short-sleeved shirt and pocket protector full of pens came over and stood beside me at the checkout counter. He was wearing geeky black glasses and had his graying hair slicked back. He was waiting for the librarian too—probably for some nerdy engineering book he'd reserved. He tapped the counter with his fingertips and looked over at me.

"Aren't you the young man who was reading to the children a minute ago?" he asked me.

"Yeah," I said. I wasn't much in the mood for talking—I was too exhausted from dealing with those little brats—so I just watched the librarian run the books under the scanner.

"Well, that's great, young man," the man with the pocket protector told me. "It's always good to see young people taking an interest in their community. What's your name, son?"

I looked up at him. He smiled. I shouldn't be rude to him, I thought. "My name's Willie," I told him. "Willie Plummet."

He held out his hand, and I shook it. "Nice to meet you, Willie," he said. Just then the librarian looked up to see who was next in line. I was relieved to cut this conversation short.

"Here's the book," I told her, setting it on the counter. "I'm done reading it to the kids."

The librarian didn't seem to notice me at all. Her eyes were on the man with the pocket protector. It was like I wasn't there. She seemed a little flustered. "Is there anything I can do for you, Mr. Van Andel?" she asked the nerdy man beside me.

"I was just wondering where the dedication ceremony was being held," Mr. Van Andel said.

"It's right over—," the librarian began to point but thought better of it. "Here, let me show you." She came out from behind the counter and led Mr. Van Andel out through the front doors, where all the people in suits had gone. I watched them disappear into the sunlight.

Slowly a smile spread across my face. The guy I thought was a nerd was really Mr. Van Andel, the millionaire philanthropist! Twice today I'd made the same mistake—judging a book by its cover.

That night, after I got my homework done, I read Luke chapter 10. I got to the part where the lawyer was talking to Jesus. The lawyer knew he was supposed to love his neighbor as himself, and he asked Jesus who his neighbor was. Jesus told the story of the Good Samaritan. Jesus' point was clear. Everyone is our neighbor—not just the people we know or like.

It hit me then that if I'd been following Jesus' words all along, I'd have plenty of things to write on my Van Andel Award form right now.

Late Saturday morning Sam showed up on my doorstep with a box full of chocolate bars. "They're only a buck-fifty each," she told me. "And they're for a good cause. We're raising money for our softball league. We're trying to fix up our playing field and put in some lights so we can play night games." Sam was a very accomplished softball pitcher.

"Come on in," I told her. "I'm good for a couple of bars. And I'll throw in a soda to boot."

Sam followed me into the kitchen, and I gave her a Coke from the refrigerator. She set the box of candy bars on the kitchen counter and hopped up to sit next to them. She popped up the tab on her can of soda and took a sip.

I pulled out my wallet and took out three $1 bills. My cash reserves were getting pretty low—thanks to those pint-sized pickpockets at the library. Sam took the money and held out a couple of chocolate bars.

"Maybe you can put this on your application for the Van Andel Award," Sam teased me. "You can claim you did volunteer work for my softball league by eating these."

I laughed and took the candy bars. "I'm not *that* desperate," I told her. "At least not anymore. I got a big break at the library yesterday."

"Yeah?" Sam said. "What happened yesterday?"

"I met him," I told Sam. "The big guy himself. I show up for *one* volunteer job at the library, and the man who's giving away the award happens to be there and sees me doing it!" I peeled back the wrapper on one of the chocolate bars. "He even came over and asked me what my name was. Can you believe it? Stephen Van Andel was right there at the library dedicating something."

Sam nodded. "I could have told you he'd be there," Sam said, stuffing my $3 into the candy box. "He was there dedicating the new high-tech room he's donating. Right?"

"Right," I said. "How did you know?" I took a bite of chocolate and held the bar out to Sam. She shook her head.

"In the newspaper," she told me. "It was in the *Glenfield Gazette*. All that stuff's in there—all the upcoming fairs and book sales and charity events are listed. And he's involved in a lot of them."

I chewed on the chocolate for a few seconds, thinking. I swallowed. "You mean, I could read the newspaper every day and find out when Mr. Van Andel will be attending some kind of ceremony?" I asked.

"Sure," Sam said. She took another sip of soda, and then it seemed to dawn on her what I had in mind. "Wait a minute," she said. "Wouldn't that be kind of cheating?"

I thought about it a moment. "I don't think it's really cheating," I said. "Every do-gooder kid in town could look up the same thing—it's a matter of public record."

Sam nodded. "Yeah, but some of the kids at the other schools have probably been working for years as volunteers," she said. "You can't come along and win the scholarship by following Mr. Van Andel around for a couple of weeks."

"What if I just happen to be doing volunteer work where he happens to be visiting every day?" I told her. "If he notices me, and ends up giving us the award, that's his business. I'm going to be working *really hard* these next few weeks. Remember the parable of the workers in the vineyard?"

"Yeah," Sam said.

"The workers who came at the very end got paid the same as the ones who had been working all day," I reminded her. "Isn't that sort of the same thing?"

Sam shook her head skeptically. "I'm not sure that really applies here," she said.

"You hear from Felix today?" I asked her, trying to change the subject.

She shook her head. "No," she said. "When's he moving in?"

"He could be here any minute," I told her. "You want to hang out and wait for him?"

She shook her head. "I've got to make my rounds with this candy, and then I'm going by the library to pick up a book on Annie Oakley," she said. She slid off the counter and picked up her box of chocolate bars. "You want me to come by later? Maybe I can help you guys move stuff."

"There's not going to be much to move," I told her. I set my unfinished chocolate bar on the kitchen counter next to the others and followed her back through the house to the front door. "He's only going to be here a couple of weeks. But come by, and we can hang out." I opened the door for her.

I was in the living room watching cartoons when the Patterson family's minivan pulled up in front of my house. I saw them through the front window. Felix got out of the passenger door and slid open the side door of the van. He brought out two small suitcases and headed across the lawn with them toward my front porch.

I opened the door for him. "You want some help with those?" I asked him as he came up the porch steps. "You want me to take them up?"

"Up to your room?" Felix asked.

"Up to *our* room," I corrected him.

Felix smiled. "Nah," he said. "Let's just leave them here for now. We can take them up later." He set the suitcases on the porch, just outside the door. "You can help me unload the rest, though," Felix said. "Mom's in kind of a hurry."

Felix turned and headed back to the open side door of the van. I followed. When I got to the van, I couldn't believe my eyes. The back two seats were crammed with junk. There were four more suitcases, a couple of duffel bags, and some cardboard boxes—and that's just what I could *see*. It looked like he was moving in permanently. "I thought you were staying two weeks," I said.

"Yeah, I know," Felix said. "But my mom said I couldn't bring any more stuff. I guess I'll just have to get by with what I've got here."

I rubbed the back of my neck. "A good-sized army could get by with what you've got here," I pointed out.

Felix looked at the stuff in the van and then back at my house. "How about we just set it all on the lawn for now," he said. "My mom really wants out of here."

It took us 20 minutes, but we got everything unloaded. When Mrs. Patterson pulled away from the curb, Felix's stuff was all spread out on the lawn. It would be a big job to lug it all upstairs. We both stood there looking at all the junk. It was overwhelming. Where to begin?

Felix puffed out his cheeks. He was already exhausted from loading all this in the van. "Well, let's get this upstairs," he said.

"There's so much junk here it looks like a big yard sale," I said.

"Don't exaggerate," Felix told me. "And this isn't junk. Everything I brought is a necessity."

I looked around me at the cluttered lawn. There were about a dozen cardboard boxes, bundles of clothes, a boom box, a computer, two reading lamps, a CD rack, and just about every useless object I'd ever seen in Felix's room, except for the big gumball machine he kept in the corner.

I sighed. "All right," I said. "Let's get started."

Felix picked up a heavy duffel bag. I squatted down and lifted a large white cardboard box at my feet.

"Careful with that," Felix warned me. "It's my gumball machine."

When we got back downstairs after the second load, a wood-paneled station wagon was parked at the curb in front of my house, right where the Patterson's van had been parked a few moments ago. An older man in Bermuda shorts and a woman with a wide-brimmed straw hat were on the lawn, picking through Felix's junk. Felix and I stood on the front porch watching them.

Felix looked at me and then back at the two people. "Excuse me," he called to them. "Can I help you with something?"

The man looked up. "Yeah," he said. "How much do you want for that telescope?"

I laughed. "This isn't a yard sale," I told him. "This is all my friend's stuff. But I'd be happy to sell you anything you want when he goes upstairs again."

We managed to lug everything up to my room before lunch, but it wasn't easy. Orville was in his room the whole time, but he refused to help us. When we were done, there wasn't much room left. I had two or three boxes stuffed under my bed, and there were another five crammed under Felix's cot. It was hard to walk around in the room because there was so much junk—in corners, under the desk, wedged on

the floor of the closet. We hung as many of Felix's
clothes in the closet as we could fit, and then folded
the rest and stacked them on top of my dresser.

I went downstairs and grabbed a couple of Cokes
from the refrigerator. The two of us sat in my room
catching our breath. I sat on my bed, and Felix sat facing me on the cot I'd made up for him. I took a sip of
Coke and looked around. I laughed and shook my
head. "You know, you don't need all this stuff," I told
him.

"Sure I do," Felix said. "All this is vital."

"Oh, yeah?" I said. "Let's see." I pulled up the flap
of a cardboard box at my feet. It was full of encyclopedias. I pulled a volume out and held it up. "So what
do you need this for?" I asked him. "You know we've
got a set of encyclopedias down in the living room."

"Yours aren't Britannicas," he said.

"Yes, they are," I told him.

He wiped the sweat from his brow with his fore-
arm. "When did you get yours?" he wanted to know.

I shrugged. "I don't know," I said. "Sometime
when I was in elementary school."

"Well, *these* encyclopedias are brand-new," Felix
announced triumphantly. "They're more up to date."
He grinned. "When it comes to schoolwork, you've
got to stay current, Willie."

I sighed and put the book back in the box. I
pulled another box out from under my bed and
peeked inside. It was full of *National Geographic*

magazines. "Okay," I said. "You can't tell me you've got newer *National Geographics* than we do. We just got one in the mail this week. What's so vital about these?" I pulled the top one out of the box and looked at the cover. It had a photo of the Galapagos Islands. It was from 1995.

Felix looked at the magazine in my hands. He took another sip of Coke and thought about it. "What if we got an assignment to do an oral report on the Galapagos Islands?" he said. "We'd *both* need to look at that issue. But because of my foresight, we'd have *two* copies, and we could both read them at the same time."

I looked at Felix. Sometimes it seemed like he was a few bricks short of a full load. Only he would cart a half-ton of *National Geographics* across town, just in case we both needed to look at the same issue at the same time.

"You know, you didn't really have to bring these," I told him. "If we had to do an oral report on the Galapagos Islands, I'd give you my 1995 copy of this very magazine." I waved the magazine in the air.

Felix eyed me suspiciously. "Yeah?" he said. "But what would *you* do?"

"I'd look up the Galapagos Islands in your brand-new encyclopedias," I told him. "When it comes to schoolwork, you've got to stay current, you know."

Just then the doorbell rang. It had to be Sam. Felix and I went downstairs and let her in. She was holding a newspaper.

"So how are the roomies?" she asked, stepping into the living room.

I glanced at Felix. "We're doing fine," I told her. "Even though Felix brought enough junk over to sink an aircraft carrier."

Felix pushed his glasses up higher on his nose. "I believe in being prepared," he said.

"I hope your folks were prepared too," she said. "You should see what's on the front page of the newspaper." She held it out to us.

Glenfield Burglar Claims New Victim
Local Family Returns from Vacation to Find House Robbed

"It's the third burglary in town in the last month," Sam said. "Two of them happened while the families were on vacation. I hope your parents took some precautions."

"Like what?" Felix asked.

"The article says to set up lights or a television on timers, so it looks like someone's at home," Sam told him. "It also says you should get a neighbor to empty your mailbox and pick up your paper every day. That's the kind of thing burglars look for."

"I don't think they did any of that stuff," Felix said. "They just told the neighbors across the street to keep an eye on the place." He looked worried. "You think we might get robbed?"

"I just thought you should know," Sam said. "It might pay to take some precautions."

Felix stared out the window anxiously. "Relax," I told him. "We can do all the stuff it says in the article. We'll go by your place every day after school and pick up the mail. We'll get some timers at the Home Warehouse and put them in this afternoon. Everything will be fine."

Felix looked at me. "Maybe Sam and I can do it," he said. "You can just stay here and watch TV. It won't take us that long." He looked down at the ground.

Sam and I both stared at him.

"Why can't *Willie* come help?" Sam asked him.

Felix sighed, still looking at the floor. "I kind of promised my parents I wouldn't let him come within 100 yards of our house," he said. "It was part of our agreement."

Sam laughed and looked at me. "I'm surprised more people don't have that policy," she said.

When Felix and Sam left, I looked through the newspaper for the calendar section to see if Mr. Van Andel had any charity events coming up. I found the

stuff I wanted on the fifth page. One of the events listed was the Annual Glenfield Community Hospital
Carnival, which was taking place tomorrow afternoon, Sunday. The listing said that all funds raised
would benefit the Van Andel Children's Wing.

It seemed like a good bet that Mr. Van Andel
would be there—and even if he weren't, it would still
make for a good addition to my application form.

I closed the paper and set it on the coffee table. I
turned on the television and found a John Wayne
movie. I watched it a few minutes and then I remembered my chocolate bars on the kitchen counter. I
was in the mood for a snack.

When a commercial came on, I went in the
kitchen. My candy bars were gone. I lifted up the lid
of the kitchen trash can. The crumpled wrappers lay
on top of the garbage.

Orville!

Annie Oakley Rides Again

When I brushed my teeth that night and went back to my room, the light was out and the window was open. I tried to get to my bed in the dark, but I stubbed my toe on one of Felix's boxes and scratched my shin on something metal. I pulled back the covers on my bed and slipped between the sheets. I was exhausted from carrying Felix's stuff upstairs. My muscles were already beginning to ache. It would be a lot worse tomorrow. I closed my eyes. A noisy car passed by outside.

"Hey, Felix," I whispered. "You still awake?"

"Yeah," he said.

"Could you close the window, please?"

There were a few seconds of silence. "I always sleep with the window open," he said. "I like the fresh air."

"Yeah," I said. "But the noise keeps me awake. Every car that goes by wakes me up if the window's open."

"But if the window is closed, I feel like I'm going to suffocate," Felix said. "It really bugs me."

I sighed. "Okay," I said, trying to hide my irritation. "We'll try it your way. But if I can't sleep, I'm going to get up and close it."

"Okay," Felix said, and a minute later he was snoring.

I rolled over and tried to get to sleep. Outside another car passed by.

"No," a voice whispered in the darkness. "Not the blue ones. Just take the ones with the spots."

My eyes shot open. I was lying facing the wall. I held my breath.

"I'm telling you it's the ones with the spots," the voice said again.

Burglars, I thought. My heart started racing. The voice was right in the room with me. I was suddenly alert and terrified. I froze and strained to hear what was going on.

"Come *on*, Willie," the voice said. "How come you never do anything right?"

Willie? What was going on here?

"You're dumb as a box of hammers," the voice said—and then it occurred to me that it was Felix's voice. I'd forgotten he was in the room with me. I rolled over and sat up in bed. I peered through the darkness at Felix's side of the room.

"What are you talking about?" I called over to Felix's cot. "What are you doing over there?"

Felix snorted and rolled over. The cot squeaked and groaned as he moved. A few seconds later he was snoring again. I lay back down on my pillow and tried to slow my heart down. Just what I needed—a sleep-talker. He'd really given me a fright. I closed my eyes and tried to swallow my anger and go back to sleep.

"Not the blue ones," Felix mumbled. "Are you some kind of idiot?"

I sat up in bed again. It was bad enough having a roommate who talked in his sleep—but having one who insulted me in his sleep was more than I could take. I shivered. The room was cold now because of the open window. He'd been here one night, and already he was ticking me off.

"Come on, Willie," Felix mumbled. "Get it through your thick skull."

I clenched my fists and shook my head. Felix wanted the window open so he wouldn't feel like he was suffocating. He didn't realize that the real danger was being suffocated by his roommate.

"Not *that* way, Willie," Felix said.

That's it! I thought. I felt on the floor beside me in the darkness and pulled the Galapagos Islands *National Geographic* from the cardboard box.

"Do I have to do everything?" Felix said. I lobbed the magazine over at his bunk. It fluttered through the air and found its mark.

"Aaaahh!" Felix yelled. "It's got me. Help!"

I suppressed a laugh. "What got you?" I asked him.

"A bat just swooped down at me," Felix said groggily. "It was huge."

"Yeah," I said. "We had an exterminator over last year, but I guess he missed a few."

Felix's cot groaned and creaked. I knew he'd just sat up in bed and was looking around. "You don't really have bats in here, do you?"

"Blue ones," I told him. "And ones with spots."

"Huh?" Felix said, still half asleep.

"They get in when you leave the window open," I told him.

"Oh," Felix said. "My bad." I heard him reach up and pull down the window. The latch clicked shut.

The guy was a few eggs short of a full carton.

On Saturday morning, I left Felix snoring in my room and went downstairs to the kitchen to grab some breakfast before I headed to the hospital to sign on as a carnival volunteer and score some points with Mr. Van Andel.

Orville was sitting at the dining room table eating cereal. "What are you doing up so early?" I asked him. "You didn't wet the bed again, did you?"

Orville looked up from shoveling cereal into his mouth. "Shut up," he told me.

"Hey," I said. "While we're engaged in this stimulating conversation, why don't you explain what happened to my chocolate bars yesterday."

Orville ignored me. He crammed another spoonful of cereal in his mouth and chewed noisily. How long could he stay mad at me?

"Those candy bars cost me $3," I told him. "I expect you to pay for them."

"I didn't see your name on them," Orville grunted. "If you leave them out, they're up for grabs. That's *my* policy."

"Come on, Orville," I told him. "You knew they were mine. You owe me $3."

Orville snorted and pushed back his chair. He stood up and took his empty bowl into the kitchen. "Like taking candy from a baby," he said, pushing through the swinging kitchen door. There was nothing I could do. The candy bars were gone, and Orville would never agree to pay for them. Being a jerk was also his policy. No wonder his girlfriend dumped him.

I was heading out the front door when I noticed Orville's wallet and keys on the entry table. I went in the living room and found a slip of paper and a pen. "I didn't see your name on this wallet," I wrote. "And since you left it out, I knew it was up for grabs. (I believe that's your policy.)" I folded the note neatly, took $3 out of the wallet, and slipped the note inside.

I ran out the front door, got my bike from the garage, and pedaled away grinning.

At the carnival, the man in charge handed me a blue ribbon that said Volunteer Staff on it and assigned me to take care of one of the booths. I pinned the ribbon on my shirt.

The booth was more of a wood-framed canvas tent. It had a high counter at the front and a big sign on the roof that said Spill the Milk. At the back of the booth were two platforms. Each platform had a pyramid of three milk bottles—but they weren't really milk bottles; they were made of a dull-looking metal and were heavy as lead. I was supposed to take tickets and hand the customers three rubber baseballs. Anyone who knocked all three bottles off one of the platforms, throwing only three balls, won one of the many stuffed toys that hung from a rack on the booth's ceiling.

It looked pretty easy, but before the carnival opened for business, I went around to the front of my booth to give it a try. I threw a total of nine balls and only managed to topple one bottle from its stand. The problem was that the bottles were so heavy, and the balls were so light. If you hit the bottles anywhere but right in the middle, the ball ricocheted off and slapped into the net at the back of the tent.

It was a lot harder than it looked, but I guess that was the point. The easier it seemed, the more people would give it a try, and the more money the hospital would raise.

At 2:00 the carnival opened. Music started playing over the loudspeakers, and people started drifting by. I noticed that TJ, the kid who helped me out at the library, was volunteering in the petting zoo behind the row of game booths. Maybe if I got a break later on, I'd go back and say hello to him.

I had to wait about 10 minutes for my first customer to arrive, a laughing man with white hair. He was trying to prove to his wife that he could still throw a baseball like he did in high school. I was rooting for him, but he spent three tickets and only managed to topple two of the bottles. He walked away laughing and rubbing his shoulder. After that, customers came in a steady stream, with few breaks in between.

As the sun was going down, I got a half-hour break. I walked around back to the petting zoo and talked to TJ, and then got a hot dog at the concession stand and went looking for Mr. Van Andel. I found him near the front entrance and passed by him several times until I was sure he'd seen me with my Volunteer Staff ribbon.

By the time I got back to my booth, it was dark, and all the carnival lights were on. Business picked up immediately. I was picking up balls and tearing up tickets like crazy. My feet were beginning to hurt. I'd had a steady stream of customers all day, but only two of them won stuffed toys.

At around 8:00, Sam and Felix walked by with Phoebe, the 8-year-old girl who lived next door to me, in tow. Phoebe had a stuffed dinosaur tucked under her arm and was eating a huge pink cotton candy.

"Step right up," I yelled, trying my best to sound like a ringmaster. "Three balls for a dollar." The three of them saw me and came over grinning.

"There you are," Sam said. "We've been looking all over for you."

I looked at Phoebe with her cotton candy and stuffed toy. "You obviously haven't been looking too hard," I said. "Where did you get that dinosaur, Pheeb? You didn't actually win one of these games did you?"

"I landed a Ping-Pong ball in a glass bowl," she said. "It wasn't that hard."

"Really?" I said, impressed. "Wow. Most of the games here are nearly impossible."

Felix shook his head. "She wasn't even *aiming* at the bowl," Felix told me. "It was an accident. She was lucky she got the ball into the right booth!"

I laughed. Phoebe blushed. "It was no accident," she said. "I have good aim."

"Well, if you're such a good shot, you should have no problem with this game," I told her. I held out a ball. "One ticket for three balls, all you have to do is knock over three bottles."

Phoebe looked at the bottles at the back of the tent. She looked down at the rubber baseball in my hand. She looked over at Sam and Felix. "It *wasn't* an accident," she told Felix. "I was *too* aiming at the bowl."

"Prove it," Felix said. "If you knock down even *one* of those bottles, I'll give you $5."

Phoebe huffed and handed the stuffed toy and cotton candy to Sam. "Hold these for me, will you?" Phoebe said. She pulled a red ticket out of her pocket and handed it to me. I tore the ticket in half and lined up three rubber balls on the counter in front of her.

The tip of Phoebe's tongue appeared in the corner of her mouth. She picked up one of the balls and took a few steps backwards. She went into some kind of weird windup—spinning her arm around and around, like she was trying to generate enough wind power to topple the bottles without actually using the ball. Suddenly she let go of the ball. It bounced off the front counter and nearly hit me on the shoulder. It slapped off the side of the booth and rolled to the back.

Felix fell to his knees laughing and choking, and I couldn't help but laugh as well. It was the worst throw I'd seen all day.

Phoebe just glared at us. She grabbed another ball. She was angry now. She stood back and went into the same weird windup. This time, when she released the ball, it actually sailed clear over the booth. I heard it bounce on the ground behind the tent.

"It *slipped*," she said. "I think the ball was moist. That throw doesn't count, does it?"

"It counts," I told her. "And I expect you to go find that ball when you're done here. It probably landed in the petting zoo."

Phoebe made a face and picked up the last ball.

"Make sure you wipe the moisture off that one," I teased her.

"Don't let them bother you," Sam said. "They probably couldn't do it either."

Phoebe stepped back and went into her windup again, this time with more vigor than ever. It was like nothing I'd ever seen before. She was flailing all over the place—it looked like she was being chased by bees.

When she let go of the ball this time, it rocketed straight up toward the ceiling of the booth. It plowed into a large stuffed teddy bear hanging from the rack. The bear dropped down on top of the pyramid of metal bottles. All three bottles tipped over. One after another they rolled off the platform and thudded to the ground. All of us just stood in silence a few seconds, looking down at the teddy bear, which now lay among the fallen bottles.

Phoebe slapped imaginary dust off her hands. "I believe you owe me another stuffed toy," she said. She turned to Felix. "And *you* owe me $5."

"But you didn't hit them with the *ball*," I told her. "That doesn't count."

"You just said I had to knock them over," Phoebe informed me. "You didn't say *how*." She turned to Felix again. "*You* didn't say how either."

"But, but—" Felix sputtered.

"She's right," Sam said. "All you guys said was that she had to knock over three bottles to win."

I just stood there shaking my head. There was no way to argue. They'd got me on a technicality. "Okay," I said. "But I'm giving you the teddy bear you maimed with the ball."

"Fair enough," Phoebe said.

I picked up the bear and handed it to her without dusting it off. She passed it on to a stunned Felix.

"Could you carry this for me?" she said. "My hands are full." She took the cotton candy and stuffed dinosaur from Sam and started to leave.

"Wait a minute," I told her. "There's still the matter of the ball you threw clean over the booth. You've got to go find it."

Phoebe looked over at Felix. "Tell you what, Felix," she said. "You go find the ball and you'll only owe me $3 instead of $5."

Felix shrugged. "Be right back," he said. I watched him jog down along the row of booths.

"Looks like you're about to lose another stuffed toy," Sam said. She nodded toward a group of boys who were sizing up my booth.

It was Vincent Espinoza and three of the other guys on the Glenfield Middle School baseball team. One of them was Jared Bird, the team's best pitcher. All of them wore their lettermen jackets. "Piece of cake," I heard Jared tell the others. "I can do this."

Jared took off his jacket and tossed it to Vincent. He came over and handed me a ticket.

"Knock all three bottles off the platform and win a prize," I said, lining three balls up in front of him on the counter. Jared picked up a ball and weighed it in his hand. He took a step back and turned sideways to the booth, like he was standing on the mound. He wrapped his big hand around the ball, finding his grip. He looked back at his friends and grinned.

Jared stepped into the pitch and threw a fast ball directly at one of the pyramids. The ball careened off the side of the bottom left bottle and bolted into the net at the back of the booth. The bottle he nicked moved about an inch, but it didn't fall. Neither did the one balanced on top.

I looked over at Sam and Phoebe; they were having fun watching. Phoebe took a bite of cotton candy.

The guys around Jared ribbed him a little as he stepped up to the counter and took the second ball. "I didn't even get to warm up," he said. He held the second ball up for them to see. "This is the one that will do it," he said. He took his position again and wound up for his second pitch. This time, the ball cleanly knocked the top bottle off the pyramid. It fell with a thud to the dirt floor.

Jared looked pleased, but he still had the two remaining bottles on the platform—and only one ball left to throw. He stepped up to the counter and grabbed the third rubber ball.

"It's the dreaded seven-ten split," one of the other baseball players said like a sports announcer.

Jared took up his position. Everyone fell silent. Jared stared down the two remaining bottles like he was trying to psych out some timid batter. He pulled the ball up to his chest with both hands and went into his windup. The third ball glanced off one of the two remaining bottles and rocketed into the net. Three throws by Glenfield's best pitcher and only one bottle knocked off the platform. The other baseball players burst out laughing.

"We didn't make it to the play-offs, and now we don't get a stuffed toy," one of them said, pretending to sulk. "I think I'm going to take up stamp collecting."

Jared was angry. "This thing is *rigged*," he insisted, pulling on his jacket. "*Nobody* could win this game."

Before I could stop her, Phoebe chimed in. "*I* did," she said. "*I* won that game." The boys around Jared hooted and laughed.

Jared glared at Phoebe. He tugged his jacket into place. "You didn't knock the three bottles over," he said. "No way."

"It's true," Sam said grinning, enjoying the joke. "She threw one ball and knocked over all three."

The other baseball players fell silent. Jared glanced around at them. He was already embarrassed at losing—and now an 8-year-old girl was telling him she succeeded where he failed. "No *girl* could do that," Jared announced with authority. "You're lying."

I could see in Sam's eyes that Jared had said exactly the wrong thing. Her eyes seemed to blaze, her brow furrowed. Guys had told Annie Oakley that no girl could shoot a gun, and she spent her whole life proving them wrong. Annie Oakley probably had that exact same expression on her face every time she squeezed the trigger. Sam leaned in close to Jared's

face. "What do you mean no girl could do that?" Sam
said.

"Haven't you ever heard the expression 'You
throw like a girl'?" Jared asked her. "There's a reason
people say that." He glanced around at the other boys.

Sam reached into her pocket and pulled out a
ticket. She's a pitcher on her softball team, and she's
just about the best athlete I know. She slapped the
ticket down on the counter in front of me.

"You sure you want to do this?" I whispered to
her. "They're a lot harder to hit than they look."

Sam's eyes blazed. "Just give me the balls, Willie,"
she said.

Just then Felix appeared out of nowhere with the
ball Phoebe had thrown over the booth. He handed it
across the counter to me. It was a bit moist.

"I had to wrestle a goat to get that ball," Felix
said.

"Oh, *ugh*," I said. I dropped the damp ball immediately and wiped my hands on my jeans.

I found three clean balls behind the counter and
lined them up in front of Sam. Felix looked at Sam
and then at all the silent boys who were watching her.
"I missed something, didn't I?" Felix said. "Everything
always happens when I'm not around."

"Just shut up and get out of the way," Phoebe told
him. He went over and stood next to her.

Sam picked up one of the balls. She squeezed it in
her hand, getting the feel of it.

Phoebe whispered to Felix, catching him up on what he'd missed.

Sam took a couple of steps away from the booth. She faced the pyramid of jugs and found her footing the way she did when she was on the mound pitching for her softball team. She pulled up, swung her arm around, and stepped into the pitch. She flung the ball underhand, and it neatly knocked the top bottle off the other two.

The bottle klunked to the table and then thudded to the ground. Phoebe clapped, and I let out the breath I'd been holding—at least Sam would do no worse than Jared.

I looked over at the guys. Vincent was smiling; he looked impressed, but the others just hovered in the back, hands in the pockets of their lettermen jackets, looking restless and anxious. Jared's jaw muscles twitched. A few seconds of tense silence passed.

"She's been reading a book on Annie Oakley," Felix said to no one in particular, as though that explained Sam's marksmanship.

"But she's throwing *underhand*," Jared complained. "I told you she'd throw like a girl."

Exactly the wrong words again. Without a word, Sam stepped up to the counter and picked up another ball.

"Don't let him get to you," I whispered.

Sam stepped back again. She pitched for a softball team, but she could also throw overhand—I'd played catch with her hundreds of times. She stood sideways to the booth, just like Jared had. She went into a windup just like Jared's. She dropped her shoulder and stepped into the pitch, and the ball rocketed at the two remaining bottles. She hit one of them fairly solidly, but it didn't tip over; it just got nudged out of place. It was now partially hidden behind the other. The ball careened up into the net.

Jared turned to the other guys. "See?" he said.

I don't know what *Jared* saw, but *I* saw a throw that was at least as good as any of his.

Phoebe stepped up and patted Sam on the back. "You can do it," she said.

Sam stepped up and took the last ball. She leaned in over the counter and squinted, studying the position of the last two bottles.

"It's do-able," I whispered to her.

Without looking at me, she nodded. She stepped back and took up her position. Every eye was on her.

Sam went into her windup again. She reached back, lifted her leg, and stepped into the pitch. The ball sailed through the air and hit the front bottle square in the middle with a rubbery *thwack*. The bottle in the back leapt off the platform and the other fell on its side. The ball bounced back out of the booth and rolled along the ground toward the feet of the boys looking on, but no one noticed. Everyone was watching—holding their breath—as the last remain-

ing bottle slowly rolled toward the edge of the platform.

When it dropped to the ground like a rock,
Phoebe squealed and jumped up and down, clapping.
Felix and I cheered. Even some of the guys on the
baseball team applauded. Jared just glared at them.

"Pick your prize, ma'am," I said. If it was up to
me, I'd have given them all to her.

Sam pointed up at a plump pink pig. I got the
stick from under the counter and unhooked it. I handed the stuffed toy across the counter to Sam. She took
it and walked over to where Jared was still standing.
She pushed it against his chest till his arms closed
around it.

"It's a gift," Sam said smiling. "Something to
remind you of the important lesson you learned
tonight." The other boys on the baseball team hooted
and laughed. Sam turned and walked away in the
direction of the Ferris wheel. Phoebe jogged to catch
up with her. Felix paused a moment and then followed them both.

"Let's find something better to do," Jared said. He
walked off in the opposite direction, still holding the
pig. All the other boys, except Vincent, followed him.

When they were gone, Vincent came up to the
booth and handed me the ball that had bounced out.
"She could pitch for the team," he told me, looking
after Sam. "She's got quite an arm."

"You'd better believe it," I told him.

6

Sidekick Wanted

All the next week, Felix kept getting on my nerves. If it wasn't his talking in his sleep, it was the way he kept sitting in a different chair every night at dinner so that the rest of us got all moved around. One night I'd be in Dad's chair, the next in my sister, Amanda's. It was very annoying.

Felix spent an hour in the bathroom every morning, using up all the hot water. And one day, when I finally got in there, my toothbrush was wet. I don't even want to think about it.

Felix kept talking while we were watching TV, and if he'd seen the program before, he'd tell me what was about to happen. "Watch this, Dude," he'd say. "This is where he reaches out from the trapdoor and grabs her foot." I could have strangled him.

I began to avoid him when I could, which wasn't easy now that we were living in the same house. When he watched television in the living room, I went

upstairs to my bedroom. When he came upstairs, I
went down to do my homework at the kitchen table.
We didn't even walk home from school together anymore—which was fine with me. Felix would head
over to his house when the final bell rang. He'd pick
up the mail and the newspaper so his house wouldn't
become a target for the Glenfield burglar.

Most afternoons, after swinging by his house,
Felix would show up on my doorstep with some other
piece of junk from his house that he couldn't live
without. A pencil sharpener maybe—one that gave a
better point than the one in my room—or a brand of
shampoo that didn't make his hair smell so funny. And
he'd add this new item to all the other junk he'd
already crammed into my room. The only good part
was that Felix brought home a newspaper every day
so I could keep track of Mr. Van Andel.

And every night we'd have the same argument
over the window. He'd want it open, and I'd want it
closed. No matter how much I reasoned with him or
yelled at him, he wouldn't close the window. I didn't
get a good night's sleep all week.

And of course the room itself made me crazy. I
couldn't stand it. Just going in there made my skin
crawl. And this was *my* bedroom—my private
domain. This was where I was supposed to go to
escape all the things that were bothering me.

All week I burned with anger and resentment.

On Thursday, I went up to the room and looked at all the junk. The least he could do was keep it all on his side of the room. I shoved some boxes over toward his cot, to make some room next to my bed. I took the books and papers stacked on my desk and stacked them on the boxes on his side of the room. I picked up the last stack of papers and was taking it over to put with the others when I stopped dead in my tracks. My mouth fell open.

"Butch Cassidy: A Legend of the West" the title on the top sheet of paper read. Beneath that it said, "By Felix Patterson."

I shuffled through the pages. It was all about Butch Cassidy—six pages worth. Felix was writing his paper on *Butch Cassidy* instead of the *Sundance Kid*. No wonder I couldn't find any books in the school library! Felix had stolen them all out from under me. I went over to my desk where I'd put the books I'd checked out of the public library. They were gone!

I stomped over to Felix's side of the room. Sure enough, next to his cot was a stack of books about Butch Cassidy—including the ones *I'd* checked out!

That was it! That was the last straw!

I heard the doorbell ring downstairs. It had to be Felix. He didn't have a key, and I'd locked the door, half-thinking I might pretend no one was home when he rang.

Gripping Felix's paper in my fist, I stomped down the stairs and across the living room to the front door. I pulled open the door and stood in the doorway, glaring at him. He held a newspaper under one arm and a cuckoo clock under the other. Sam was with him. Felix saw my expression and took a few steps backwards.

"What is the meaning of this?" I growled. I waved Felix's paper in the air in front of my face.

Felix shrugged. "I think it means you surrender," he said.

I was about to explode. "This isn't a white flag, you idiot," I told him. "It's some stupid paper on Butch Cassidy."

Felix grinned. "Really?" he said. "Did you read it? What did you think?"

"I didn't read it," I shouted. "But what's more important, I didn't *write* it."

"Of course you didn't write it," Felix said. "Why would you write *my* paper?"

I was so angry, I think I did an involuntary little dance right there in the doorway. "This isn't *your* paper," I yelled. "It's *my* paper. Only *you* wrote it."

"You're not making any sense, Dude," Felix said. "If *I* wrote it, how could it be *your* paper?"

"Because it's *my* subject," I told him. "*I'm* writing on Butch Cassidy."

"*Your* subject?" Felix said. "*I'm* the one writing on Butch Cassidy."

"You're writing on the *Sundance Kid*," I shouted. "We agreed on that weeks ago."

"We agreed to write on Butch and Sundance," Felix said. "I assumed *you'd* be Sundance."

"Well, you assumed wrong," I yelled.

"You guys," Sam interrupted. I'd pretty much forgotten she was there. "You think maybe we could take this inside? Is this something the whole neighborhood needs to hear?"

I looked across the street. Mrs. Walker, who had been weeding her lawn, was standing and watching us. I stepped back into the living room. Felix came inside and Sam pulled the door shut behind her. Felix set the cuckoo clock and the newspaper on the coffee table. We stood a few awkward seconds in silence there in the living room, both waiting for the other to start up the argument again.

"Okay," Sam said. "How are we going to sort this out so we can all be friends again?"

"I don't know if I *want* to be friends with Felix anymore," I said. "The little spaz is driving me nuts."

"Well, let's be fair about this," Felix said. "If one of us has to start over with his paper, it should be the one who's done the least work. I've written six pages. How many pages have you written?"

I just stood there. The truth was I hadn't even started my paper. The truth was I hadn't even started reading the books. I'd been too busy doing volunteer work and being angry with Felix. But that didn't seem to be the point right then. Butch was the main guy, and Sundance was his sidekick. I didn't want to be the sidekick. Sam and Felix both watched me, waiting for me to answer.

"It's not the number of pages," I said more to Sam than to Felix. "It's the principle of the thing. First he takes over my room. Then he takes my library books. Then he takes Butch Cassidy." I looked at Felix and then back at Sam. "It's like he's taking over my life."

"Moving in here was *your* idea," Felix pointed out. "I was just going to stay with my aunt."

I turned to face Felix. "Okay," I said. "Maybe this whole thing was a mistake, but something's got to change before I go crazy."

"Like what?" Felix wanted to know.

"If we've got to share a room," I said. "We're going to have to set some boundaries."

Felix rubbed his chin suspiciously. "What kind of boundaries?"

"We'll put a masking tape line down the middle of the room. You, and all your precious stuff, will stay on your side of the line. The other side of the line is all mine."

Sam sighed and shook her head. We both ignored her.

"What about the stuff we *share*?" Felix asked.

"Like what?"

"Like the desk."

"We'll put a line down the middle of that too," I said. "Your papers and books can go on your side and my stuff will go on mine."

"What about Sam?" Felix asked. "She's still our best friend."

"Oh, no," Sam said. "You're not putting masking tape on me."

"We'll take turns," I said. "You'll get Sam on Mondays, Wednesdays, and Fridays. I'll get her on Tuesdays, Thursdays, and Saturdays."

"What about Sundays?"

I shrugged. "Maybe that can be her day off."

"I have a better plan," Sam said. "You can both leave me out of this until you grow up."

"But we're your best friends," Felix said. "Which one of us are you going to hang out with?"

Sam looked back and forth between Felix and me. "Maybe I'll just hang out with Phoebe," Sam said. "At least she's *supposed* to act like an 8-year-old."

When our argument wound down, Felix went upstairs with the cuckoo clock. I gave him one hour to get all his stuff over to his side of the room. Then I'd come upstairs with the masking tape.

I sat down on the sofa, still fuming. Sam sat on the sofa too, but as far from me as she could. She didn't seem too pleased with me.

I turned on the television, just so there'd be some noise, and then I noticed the newspaper on the coffee table. I picked it up, shook it out, and looked at the front page. **Glenfield Burglar Claims Sixth Victim**, the lead article read. **Thief Considered Armed and Dangerous**.

I opened the paper and looked for the calendar of upcoming events. I couldn't believe it. There on the fifth page was a whole article on Stephen Van Andel—**Software Giant Donates Time, Money**. At the top was a photograph of him handing someone an oversized check. The article told all about Mr. Van Andel's charitable work in Glenfield. It not only mentioned the library and the hospital—it also mentioned the upcoming Pet Expo to raise money for the animal shelter, Mr. Van Andel's planned visit to the soup kitchen, and his ongoing prison ministry.

"Looking for more volunteer work?" Sam asked suddenly. I was surprised she was still talking to me.

"Yeah," I said.

"Remember the second most important commandment?" she asked me.

I put the newspaper down on my knee and looked over at her. "Yeah," I said. "'Love your neighbor as yourself.'"

Sam nodded. "And who's your closest neighbor right now?"

I felt my cheeks turn red. I knew what she meant. I was going out of my way to help out complete strangers, but I wasn't even willing to cut Felix, my best friend and roommate, any slack.

I pretended to watch TV. I knew Sam was right, but I didn't want to admit it. I wanted to stay angry. I told myself that Sam didn't understand. She didn't realize how hard Felix was to live with. She didn't realize how stubborn and self-centered the guy could be. This whole thing was *his* fault.

I didn't say a word. I just stared at the television and felt my stomach churn.

When Sam went home, I went in the kitchen and called the number for the animal shelter. I asked the woman who answered the phone if they needed any volunteers for the Pet Expo. I told her what an animal lover I was. She signed me up.

"We also need a permanent volunteer for Thursday afternoons," the woman told me. "Would you be interested in that?"

"No thanks, ma'am," I told her politely. "I'm pretty busy. I'd better just come for that one day."

I asked her for directions and jotted the address of the animal shelter on one of the yellow Post-it note pads Mom keeps by the phone.

Next I called the soup kitchen.

"Yeah, we need volunteers that night," the man said. "But what we really need is someone who can pick up some food. You don't have access to a truck, do you?"

"Yes," I said. "My brother, Orville, has a truck."

"Well, the Bargain Barn Grocery is donating a bunch of food. We need someone to go pick it up that night. You think you can manage that?"

"Sure," I said. "I can do that." I tore off another yellow Post-it note and took down the address to the grocery store. I slipped both addresses in my pocket and went upstairs to Orville's room.

"Orville, you've got to help me," I told him, standing in the doorway to his room. He was lying on his bed, listening to his Walkman. He was probably listening to brokenhearted love songs, I thought. Even across the room I could hear the tinny music coming from the headphones. He looked over at me and pulled the headphones down around his neck.

"I need to use your pickup truck," I told him. "It's really important."

Next door, in my room, I heard faint bumping and thumping noises. Felix was struggling to move all his stuff over to his side of the room.

Orville sat up and dropped his legs over the side of the bed. "Important, huh?" he said. "What's up?"

"It's a good cause," I told him. "I'm going to volunteer at the soup kitchen on Sunday, and I need to pick up a donation of groceries. I need your truck."

"Does this have anything to do with that stupid Van Andel Award?" Orville said. "You never seemed interested in the homeless until you thought you could get something out of it."

He had me. It was true. I never would have volunteered at the soup kitchen if it hadn't been for the grant my school might get. "That's not true," I told Orville. "I might have started out volunteering because of the award, but now I've learned a valuable lesson."

Next door Felix groaned loudly, like he'd just lifted something heavy. He probably could have used some help, but I wasn't about to volunteer.

I looked at Orville. "I've learned a valuable lesson," I repeated. "Volunteering is very rewarding. It's our duty as Christians to help those in need. 'Love your neighbor as yourself.'"

Something smashed next door. Felix yelped. I tried my best to ignore all the noise he was making.

"By helping me, you'll also be helping others," I told Orville, laying it on as thick as I could.

Orville nodded thoughtfully. It seemed like my words were getting through to him. "All you need is for me to drive you to the grocery store and then over to the soup kitchen?"

I couldn't believe it. Orville was actually going to help me. I nodded. "That's all I need," I told him.

Orville nodded again. "Well, I've got another valuable lesson for you," he said. "Stay out of your brother's wallet if you expect him to do you any favors." He pulled the headphones back over his ears and lay back on the bed.

My face stung like it had been slapped. I should have known better. Orville would be no help whatsoever. "Well, that's just like you," I told him. "You're so self-centered, you're never willing to help anyone in need." Orville stared up at the ceiling, his foot moving in time with the music, but I knew he could hear me. "There'll be snow in the Sahara before *you* ever lift a finger to help anyone," I shouted from the doorway.

Something thumped against the wall next door. Orville ignored me. I went downstairs to see what was on TV.

That night I sat on my bed with my arms crossed. I wanted to go to sleep, but cars kept passing by outside, keeping me awake. I could see the masking tape line down the middle of the room in the moonlight that came through the open window. I'd made the mistake of placing the line so that the window was on *Felix's* side—so, of course, the window was open.

On my side of the masking tape line everything was neat and tidy. But Felix's side was packed tight with leaning stacks of boxes and papers and books. In the darkness it looked like the skyline of a huge city.

Another car passed by outside. I could tell by the fact that Felix wasn't snoring (or insulting me) that he was awake too—but I wasn't about to talk to him. I might never talk to him again. He was no longer my best friend. He was no longer my sidekick.

No Animals Were Harmed in the Writing of This Chapter

On Saturday morning, the folks at Caring Friends Animal Shelter were happy to see me. This was the biggest day of the year—their Pet Expo—and their regular volunteer staff was spread pretty thin. I followed Mrs. Houston around as she made sure everything was ready. She was the director of the shelter, and she seemed anxious that everything went well today.

The parking lot and front lawn were covered with tables and displays. There was a little stage with a microphone. About a dozen volunteers were scrambling to get everything ready. When she'd made the rounds, Mrs. Houston took me back to the adoption office. It was off to the side and far from all the action.

"Since everything is going on outside, it will probably be pretty quiet in here," Mrs. Houston told me. "It's unlikely that we'll have any adoptions today. The

people who come to the Expo are already pet own-
ers."

I looked around the office; it was nothing fancy.
It had a long counter. Behind it were lots of pictures
of animals and a couple of charts that showed all the
different breeds of dogs and cats. The whole place
smelled like a wet cocker spaniel.

"Do you think you could handle any customers
who come in?" Mrs. Houston asked me. "There may
not be any visitors, but we really should keep the
office open."

"No problem," I told her. "I wait on customers at
my family's hobby shop all the time."

Mrs. Houston showed me all the paperwork that
had to be filled out for adopting a pet. She took me
through the door behind the counter and showed me
the numbered rows of cages out back where all the
animals were kept. She said she'd be out front if I
needed her.

"Is Mr. Van Andel here yet?" I asked her as she
was heading out the door.

She turned and looked back in, silhouetted
against the bright doorway. "Yes," she told me. "He's
been here all morning. He's our biggest benefactor."

"You think I might get to meet him?" I asked her.

"That can probably be arranged," she told me.

When Mrs. Houston left, I stood behind the
counter eagerly waiting for my first customer.

For the first hour, the only person who came in was a woman who wanted to know if there was a restroom in the office. There wasn't.

The next hour passed without a single visitor. I wished I'd brought a book. I'd looked at every picture and read every flyer in the office. I studied the charts of dog and cat breeds. Volunteer work could be pretty boring. When my first actual customer came in, and the bell over the door jingled, I was lying on the counter looking up at the ceiling.

"Excuse me," I told the man, rolling down off the counter. I could feel myself blush. "How can I help you?"

The man was looking for a dog. "A big dog," he told me. "The bigger the better. I grew up with a St. Bernard. Do you have any of those?" I asked him to wait a moment while I went back to check.

When I walked along the rows of cages, the dogs all barked and wagged their tails at me. There were two or three of them in each concrete-floored enclosure. They all looked healthy, but also lonely somehow. I felt good knowing that I might find one of them a home. In the first three rows, the biggest dog I found was one that looked like a small black Labrador—it was nowhere near the size of a St. Bernard.

I started down the fourth and final row of cages, feeling a little disappointed. Maybe I wouldn't get to help any of these dogs after all. None of them were very large.

I came around the corner of the last row and found two huge dogs chained to the side fence. They were the biggest dogs I'd ever seen in my life—so big they wouldn't have fit in the normal enclosures. Both were black with droopy faces and pointed ears. As I came up to them they both stood and watched me, their heads low, their tails wagging. I could have saddled them up and ridden them home if I'd wanted to.

I love dogs—I've grown up around them—but with a dog you don't know, it pays to be careful. I edged closer to the giant animals. "Nice puppies," I said, a nervous smile plastered on my face. "You wouldn't eat a Van Andel Award nominee, would you?"

I stopped when I got close enough to touch them. They strained at their chains and writhed and wriggled, trying to reach me—to lick me or eat me. Their heads were about the same height as my chest. If they stood on their hind legs they'd be taller than me.

"Nice puppies," I said again. "Sit, puppies."

The moment the words left my mouth, the two dogs plopped their rear ends down on the concrete. I stood a moment sizing up the situation. "Lie down," I tried. The two huge dogs dropped to the floor obediently. I furrowed my brow and looked down at them. Someone had trained these dogs well. "Stay," I told them.

I kept a close eye on the dogs as I carefully stepped between them. Their long, wagging tails swept the concrete floor. I unlatched the chains from the fence and stepped back holding the ends. "Okay," I said. "Come on." The two huge dogs rose to their feet and walked on either side of me all the way back to the office.

They didn't pull on their leashes like my own dog, Sadie, does when I walk her—and it was a good thing; I could never have held them back. Instead, the huge dogs kept pace with me, always looking straight ahead. They were the best-behaved dogs I'd ever seen. I really hoped I'd find one of them a good home.

When I brought the two dogs around the counter, the man couldn't believe his eyes. "They're beautiful," he said. "I wasn't expecting anything like this. What kind of dogs are these?"

I glanced up at the chart on the wall. Down at the bottom was a dog that looked just like these two. I stepped closer and read the name. "Great Danes," I said. "I think they're Great Danes."

"They're beautiful," the man said. "How could dogs like these end up here?"

I shrugged. "Maybe something happened to their owner," I guessed. "Someone took good care of them. They seem to be well trained." I looked down at the dogs. "Sit," I told them. They instantly dropped to a sitting position. "Lie down," I said. They stretched out on the floor. The man was beside himself with excitement.

"Do you think I could take both of them?" he asked. I glanced around the office, but of course no one was there. I thought of going out to find Mrs. Houston, but I knew she'd be busy. Besides, I figured that finding a home for two dogs was even better than finding a home for one. I looked down at the Great Danes. They seemed to have been together a long time. Why split them up now?

"Sure," I told him. "I don't know why you can't take both of them."

I found the necessary forms and filled out all the information they called for while the man knelt on the floor and played with the huge dogs. The dogs licked his face, their tails wagging. I asked him the questions for each space on the form, and he answered them, when he could manage to stop laughing. When I was done, the man signed the form and got out his checkbook. He paid the fees, and I handed him the chains.

"I'm glad we could help you," I told him, holding the office door open so he and his new dogs could pass through. He was beaming with happiness as he led his Great Danes out to his car—and they followed him obediently.

As I watched him pull out of the parking lot, I felt good. I'd helped find those two huge dogs a good home.

In the next 20 minutes not a single person came in the office. I began to wonder when Mrs. Houston was coming back. I couldn't wait to tell her the good news about the two Great Danes.

Around 4:00, Mrs. Houston came blustering in. "You wanted to meet Mr. Van Andel," she said, before I had a chance to speak. "Well, here's your big chance."

"Cool," I said. "Is he coming in here?" I started smoothing back my hair with my fingers. I wanted to make a good second impression.

"No," she said. "He's not coming in here. I told him you'd take him his dogs."

I came out from behind the counter, tucking my shirt into my jeans. "He wants to adopt some dogs?" I asked.

"No," she said, laughing. "His *own* dogs. A pair of champion Great Danes. We tied them up out back about an hour ago. He's going to do an obedience demonstration."

I swallowed. "Great Danes?" I said.

"Black ones," she said, trying to shoo me toward the back door. "Go on out back. You can't miss them; they're the size of horses. And hurry. Mr. Van Andel is waiting."

She'd scooted me halfway out the back door before I regained the power of speech. "Mrs. Houston," I managed to say. "We have a problem."

A Cold Day in the Sahara

In an odd way, I'd gotten my wish. Mr. Van Andel knew my name. I'd be amazed if he ever forgot it: Willie Plummet—the knucklehead who gave away his champion dogs.

Actually, Mr. Van Andel wasn't as angry as he might have been. He seemed to understand it was an honest mistake, and when I called the dogs' new owner on the phone and explained the situation, he brought the Great Danes right back. The only thing it cost me was a big dose of embarrassment.

"I guess I should take it as a compliment," Mr. Van Andel told me as he put his dogs in the back of his green Land Rover. "My dogs were here for just a few minutes and someone adopted them. I guess you have a good eye for dogs, Willie."

When I got up to my room late that afternoon, it had twice as much junk as it had when I left that morning. I couldn't even open the door all the way; it bonked against a crate full of comic books. When I squeezed through the half-open door, I felt like screaming. There was junk covering the entire floor. I couldn't see the masking tape line anymore—I couldn't even see the carpet.

There was a television, another stereo, a rack of video games, a set of golf clubs, about a dozen new boxes, an aquarium full of goldfish, and, of all things, a toaster oven. I couldn't believe it. What was Felix thinking?

I stomped downstairs to the living room where Felix slouched in front of the television. He was sprawled on the sofa, watching Cartoon Network. He seemed to be in a television stupor. He didn't even see me coming. As I got close to him, I could see the Jetsons reflected in his glasses. I stepped between him and the television. Felix looked up at me, confused.

"What is all that junk up in my room?" I shouted.

"Dude, there's a burglar out there," Felix said, gesturing behind him at the window. "I'm taking precautions. My house is a sitting duck. Everyone on the block knows no one is living there."

"But how did you manage to get it all here?" I said.

"Your brother helped me move it in his truck," Felix told me. "He said to tell you there's a big cold front in the Sahara today—whatever that means."

Orville! I slapped my forehead. I'd told him there'd be snow in the Sahara the day he lifted a finger to help someone—and who does he choose to help? Felix! I just couldn't believe he'd go to so much trouble just to get back at me. What a jerk! No wonder he got dumped!

Felix leaned to one side, so he could watch the Jetsons around me. I was furious. I stepped in front of him again. "I can't live with all that junk lying around," I shouted. "It's a blatant violation of the Masking-Tape Agreement."

Felix shook his head like I was being unreasonable. "Dude, all that stuff's *valuable*," he informed me. "It's just the kind of stuff burglars are always stealing."

"*Goldfish*?" I shouted.

"Well, not the goldfish," Felix admitted. "But they looked kind of lonely once all the other stuff was gone."

"I want that stuff out of my room," I told him. "I want the Masking-Tape Agreement reinstituted."

"Dude, there was no way to get all that stuff on my side of the room," Felix said. "It isn't reasonable."

Reasonable? I clenched my fists. The word *reasonable* didn't belong in Felix's vocabulary. He was definitely a few fries short of a Happy Meal.

I glared down at him. He leaned farther over to see the television around me. I'd had it. I couldn't take any more. "Felix," I said. "You and I are no longer friends."

That night I lay in bed listening to Felix snore. I felt claustrophobic with all the shadowy stacks of junk around me. To make it worse, the window was open; I could feel the cool, unpleasant breeze. At that moment I wished I had never met Felix—wished he'd never been born. I hadn't spoken to him since our argument in the living room. Even at dinner, when we all sat around the table in the wrong places, I refused to admit he existed. Somehow my best friend had become my worst foe.

The next morning I ignored Felix all through Sunday school. He sat in the front row, and I sat in the back. I waited until he left the room before I got out of my chair.

When I got to the church sanctuary for the service, Felix was sitting in the sixth row on the right side of the center aisle, where Sam and I usually join him. He glanced back and saw me coming down the center aisle, but he quickly turned and faced forward again, pretending he hadn't seen me.

I paused a moment, wondering what to do. I know I was right there in church, and my mind should have been on holier things, but it wasn't. I know I should have acted out of love for my neighbor, but I didn't. All I could think of was my room full of Felix's junk, his half-finished report on Butch Cassidy, and all the sleep I'd lost since Mr. I-Must-Have-The-Window-Open had moved in. I looked down the center aisle at the front of the church. I could almost imagine a masking-tape line running down along the carpet, splitting the church in half. Felix glanced over his shoulder again.

Knowing he was watching me, I walked down the center aisle, passed him, and entered a pew on the left. I sat next to TJ Drew. He seemed glad to see me. He scooted over a little so I'd have more room. I leaned over and chatted with him while people filled the church around us. As I spoke to TJ, I imagined Felix, sitting behind us by himself, wondering if I had found a new best friend, a new Sundance Kid.

When it was almost time for the service to start, I glanced back to see if Felix was watching me with TJ. He was still alone in his pew. Behind him a few rows,

Sam was sitting next to Phoebe. I should have known Sam wouldn't choose sides—but sitting next to Phoebe seemed a little extreme.

The pastor made some announcements, but I didn't listen. My mind was on other things. *Was this how it would end?* I thought. Were all those years of friendship over? I thought back on all the things the three of us had been through together: we'd set off a UFO scare, we'd started our own band, and we'd survived countless mishaps and misadventures. Was that all behind us?

I glanced back at Felix as the organ music started; he pretended elaborately not to notice me. I thought about his insults when he was talking in his sleep. Was that how he really thought of me? My heart went hard. I could find a new best friend.

We stood to sing a hymn, and I shared a hymnal with TJ. I listened to his deep voice as he sang. He really might make a good best friend, I thought. He was three years older than I was. It would be a big boost in status for me to have a best friend who went to high school. No more hanging around pipsqueaks like Felix!

And then it hit me. TJ had a pickup truck. With him as a friend, I didn't need to make up with Orville, either!

That's it, I thought. I now have a new best friend.

I looked over at TJ as we sang the last verse of the hymn. I smiled at him. He smiled back.

When TJ and I passed by the soup kitchen that night, Mr. Van Andel's green Land Rover was already parked out front. "Whoa," I said. "Turn around. He's there already. If we pick up the food now, I might miss him."

TJ drove up to the corner and made a U-turn. He pulled his truck up behind Mr. Van Andel's. "Look," I said. "I need to make sure he sees me here before he leaves. Could you go on and pick up the food and bring it back here?"

TJ glanced at his watch. "Okay," he said. "I guess."

I reached into the pocket of my jacket and pulled out a yellow Post-it note. "Here's the address," I told him. "Just go around to the back door and tell them you're there to pick up the food. They'll know what you mean."

TJ looked at the address on the paper. "Sure thing," he said. I got out and slammed the door. TJ backed up and then pulled out into traffic. I watched him go down to the corner and make another U-turn. When he passed by on the far side of the road, I waved to him. He'd volunteered to help me at the soup kitchen without any argument. He was making an excellent new best friend.

I turned and looked up at the doors of the soup kitchen. I ran my fingers back through my hair and pulled down the hem of my jacket. I climbed the steps and pushed open the door.

All night, as I helped out, back in the kitchen, I made every excuse I could to come out to the serving line, hoping Mr. Van Andel would see me. I was back in the kitchen washing dishes when TJ came back to help.

"You got the food?" I asked him, running a soapy sponge around the inside of a bowl.

"No problem," TJ said. "I just pulled up and they loaded it on. It's parked outside, right in front of that Land Rover. What's it all for?"

I ignored his question; my mind was on other things. "Is Mr. Van Andel still out there?" I asked.

"He was just getting ready to leave," TJ told me. "Why?"

I threw down my sponge. "I'll explain later," I told TJ. "I've got to catch him before he goes." I raced out of the kitchen, just as Mr. Van Andel was going out the door.

"Mr. Van Andel," I called. "It's good to see you again."

He turned and came back in the room. He didn't seem to recognize me.

"How are your dogs?" I asked him. I knew that would jog his memory.

"Why, it's Willie Plummet, isn't it?" he said, smiling now. "I thought I saw you here. My dogs are fine. I've managed to hold on to them another day," he joked.

I laughed more loudly than his little joke called for. There were a few seconds of tongue-tied silence. I just stood there, grinning like an idiot.

"I seem to see you everywhere these days," Mr. Van Andel said.

"Well, I just love to volunteer," I told him. "Nothing like helping out those less fortunate."

"Well, good to see you again," he said. He turned to the door.

"I also brought some food," I blurted out. Mr. Van Andel turned to look at me again. "A whole truckload," I said. "It's parked right out front. Nothing fancy, just nutritious." I tried to make it sound like maybe I'd donated all the food myself. I knew that was wrong, but I was getting desperate.

"That's very impressive, Willie," Mr. Van Andel told me. "It's wonderful to see a young man working so hard to make a difference."

"Oh, it's nothing," I said. "Anything to help the community."

Mr. Van Andel smiled and nodded. "Well," he said. "I really must be going. Keep up the good work." He turned and went out the door.

I just stood there as the door swung shut behind him. He'd said he was very impressed. He remembered my name. The truck was parked right in front of his Land Rover; he couldn't miss it. Better rearrange the furniture in the school library, I thought. Make room for the computers!

"That sure felt good," TJ told me as we left the soup kitchen an hour later. "The grateful look on the faces of those hungry people—it was wonderful."

"Volunteer work does have its rewards," I said. We walked down the front steps.

"I think I'd like to come back here," TJ said as we turned and headed down the street toward his truck. "I think I'd like to do this again."

"We're not done yet," I told him. "We still have to take that food around back."

"Back where?" TJ asked.

I looked down the street at his pickup. It was lit up brightly under the streetlight. "To the back of the building, of course," I said. As we came up next to the truck, I imagined how impressed Mr. Van Andel must have been when he passed by and saw it so full of Dog Chow.

Dog Chow?

I stood there blinking. The back of TJ's truck was loaded down with 50-pound bags of Dog Chow. *Nothing fancy*, I'd told Mr. Van Andel. *Just nutritious.*

"What have you done?" I yelled at TJ. "I just told Mr. Van Andel I was going to feed all those poor homeless people dog food."

"Why did you tell him that?"

I stood there blinking, trying to form words. "I don't get it," I said. "Why did the grocery store give you a bunch of dog food?"

"Grocery store?" TJ asked me. "What grocery store?" He pulled the yellow Post-it note from his pocket and held it up for me to see.

Caring Friends Animal Shelter, it said in my own handwriting. Beneath that was the animal shelter's address.

I felt in my pocket and pulled out another yellow Post-it note. On it was written the address of the Bargain Barn Grocery. I slapped my forehead and then dragged my hand down my face. I'd given TJ the wrong slip of paper! And I'd told Mr. Van Andel that I was planning to feed dog food to the less fortunate citizens of Glenfield!

I was standing on the sidewalk, but I felt like I was on an express elevator to the basement.

That night I lay on my bed awake and angry. I'd probably blown the Van Andel Award, and now I was sitting in a cold room that was overrun with junk. A car passed by the open window. Tomorrow was Monday, a school day; I couldn't afford to be losing sleep like this. Felix, to whom I hadn't spoken in a couple of days, was snoring contentedly in his cot.

Something had to be done. As I lay there fuming, I began to formulate a plan. I'd have to think of some way to get TJ to help me. I could count on TJ. He was a very helpful guy. My plan was shaping up.

The Plan I Formulated

On Tuesday afternoon I sat on the front porch doing homework. It was the only way to be sure I could avoid Felix.

I looked up from the book I was reading to see Sam coming down the sidewalk in my direction. It was good to see her. I really missed her since we'd stopped hanging out.

"Man, am I glad to see you," I told her when she was close enough to hear.

She smiled awkwardly and looked at the house next to mine. "Actually, I was on my way to Phoebe's," she said. "She's expecting me." She started to walk past.

"Well, hang on a minute," I begged her. "What's been happening? What are you up to these days?" I just wanted to talk to her.

She thought a moment. "Well, they've started putting up the lights at the softball field," Sam said.

"And Vincent Espinoza invited me to play baseball with the guys tomorrow."

"Really?" I said. The conversation was kind of strained for two people who knew each other as well as Sam and me. "Well, that's kind of exciting."

Sam smiled and tucked her blond hair behind her ears. "Kinda," she said.

She looked at me, and I looked at her. Neither of us said anything.

"Well," Sam said finally. "Phoebe's expecting me."

"See you later," I called after her as she passed on to Phoebe's house.

"See ya'," she called back to me.

"You're sure you don't want to come with us to the movie?" Mom asked me at the dinner table that night. "I thought you really wanted to see this one."

There was no way I was going to the movie tonight. *Felix* was going.

But there was another reason too. When they all left, I'd be alone in the house. This would be the perfect opportunity to carry out my plan.

I looked over at Felix. He gnawed his way along a piece of corn on the cob. "Actually, I was looking forward to some time *alone*," I said, still looking at him pointedly. "I've got a lot to do on my *Butch Cassidy project*."

I got no reaction from Felix; he was too immersed in his own little project—getting every last kernel of corn off the stupid cob.

"Well, you'd better get your project done before this weekend," Mom warned. "You know Grammie is expecting us at her house on Saturday for the twins' birthday party."

"Yeah," I said. "Sure thing."

I waited until the car drove away before I called TJ. I gave him the story I'd worked out, and then I went up to my room with a screwdriver. The house was deliciously empty and quiet. I scrambled over all the junk in the room to Felix's cot. I crawled along the cot to the window. I loosened a couple of screws on the window frame. I pulled up the window. It stayed open for maybe half a minute and then suddenly slid down shut again. I pulled it back up. This time it only stayed up a few seconds before it fell and clicked shut. I smiled. No more open windows in this room!

By the time I put the screwdriver back in the garage, TJ's pickup was already out front.

"You're sure it's okay to put all that stuff back in Felix's house?" TJ asked as we carried the first load down the stairs to his waiting truck. "Are you sure Felix wants us to do this? Haven't you heard there's a burglar loose around here?"

"Believe me," I said. "I've heard plenty about the burglar. But I've got a big old padlock. We'll just put the junk in the garage and lock it up. It will be perfectly safe."

It took us about half an hour, but we carried load after load out to TJ's truck. I knew even then that what I was doing was wrong, but I told myself I was only enforcing the Masking-Tape Agreement. I was only going to clear off my side of the room.

When the truck was full, we tied all the junk down with twine so it wouldn't fall out if we made a sharp turn. TJ tied the loose end of the twine to one of the cleats on the side of his truck bed. He plucked the twine like a guitar string; it was snug.

It was dark and cold, but both of us were sweating from our exertion. TJ wiped his forehead with the hem of his T-shirt. He was a good friend. He was really willing to go out of his way to be of assistance. I was amazed by how hard he worked to help me out—of course *he* thought it was Felix he was helping.

We got in the pickup and pulled away from the curb. I rolled down the window and felt the cool breeze on my sweaty face.

At Felix's house we backed into the driveway. TJ hopped out first and slammed his door.

"Shhh," I whispered through the open window.

TJ looked in at me, puzzled.

"His neighbors go to bed very early," I lied. "I promised Felix we'd be very quiet."

TJ nodded. "Sorry," he whispered.

I got out of the truck quietly. TJ pulled a pocketknife from his jeans and opened it. He cut the twine while I pulled open the garage door. We started to unload.

"Why didn't Felix come along to help us?" TJ whispered as we both carried a large box of books to the back of the Pattersons' dark garage.

"He had something else to do," I grunted. We both squatted and set the box down. "But I'm sure he really appreciates what we're doing for him." I straightened up and turned back toward the open garage door. "A couple more trips, and—"

At that instant the lights hit us. There must have been a half dozen spotlights that blinded us from every side.

"Keep your hands in the air," a voice boomed menacingly over some kind of loudspeaker. "Come slowly out of the garage."

"No! No!" I said from the backseat of the police car. "You've got it all wrong. *We're* not the burglars. My friend *lives* in that house." The cop who was driving ignored me.

I looked over at TJ. He was staring straight ahead with his brow furrowed. He looked like he was in shock.

"This is nothing," I assured him. "When my folks get home with Felix everything will get straightened out. We'll only be in jail a few hours." TJ's expression didn't change, and he didn't look over at me. "Everything's going to be okay," I told him. "Stuff like this happens to me all the time."

TJ's head turned slowly to look at me. It was as if he was in a trance. Lights from passing traffic moved across his expressionless face. He stared at me a moment like I had just now appeared in the seat beside him. "You know, Willie," he said, like he had given it a great deal of thought. "I don't think I really want to be your best friend anymore."

Forty-five minutes later TJ and I were in a holding cell. I stood at the bars, trying to find out from one of the passing deputies whether my parents were on their way yet. TJ lay on the bunk facing the wall. He seemed depressed. I wished I could cheer him up.

"You don't talk in your sleep, do you?" I asked him. "My last roommate talked in his sleep." I laughed at my own joke.

TJ didn't move.

"They'll be home in a few minutes," I assured him. "They'll hear our message on the answering machine, and they'll come right over to straighten everything out."

TJ didn't respond.

"This'll be a great story," I went on. "Someday we'll look back on this and laugh."

TJ still said nothing.

"It's really funny when you think about it," I said. "We get arrested for being the Glenfield Burglar. They think we're criminal masterminds. It's a riot."

TJ didn't stir.

"Talk to me, TJ," I begged. "Aren't you going to say *anything*?"

TJ rolled over to look at me. "I don't want to be your best friend anymore," he told me, and he rolled back to face the wall.

Well, I'd done it. I'd managed to lose three best friends in one week. At this rate I'd go through 84 new best friends by Christmas! I turned and looked out of the cell again. What a day!

A deputy walked by outside the bars. "Sir?" I said. "Sir?" He didn't even glance in. He walked down to the far end of the corridor where I couldn't see him; I heard a steel door creak open. I heard some voices, and then someone yelled "Visitor!" The steel door clanged shut again.

It had to be my dad. I felt like dancing. I glanced over at TJ. He was still facing the wall. "We're out of here, TJ," I said. "My dad's here." TJ didn't move.

I heard Dad's footsteps coming down the row of cells, accompanied by one of the guards. I pressed my face to the bars, trying to see. Out of the corner of my eye I could see him coming.

"Man, am I glad to see you!" I called out to him. "You won't *believe* what happened to—"

I stopped mid-sentence. It wasn't my dad. I was suddenly face to face with Mr. Van Andel.

My mind raced. *Of course!* I thought. *His prison ministry!* I felt like banging my head on the bars.

Mr. Van Andel stood there blinking, stunned to find someone he knew in jail. "Willie?" he said. "Willie Plummet?"

I plastered an awkward smile on my face and tried to think of something to say. "So," I blurted out. "How are the dogs?"

It took him a few seconds to formulate an answer. His lips moved a few seconds, but no sound came out. "The dogs are fine," he finally managed to say, the same stunned expression on his face. And then he was gone.

I turned and leaned back on the cold bars of the holding cell. I dragged my hand down my face. This was not working out the way I'd planned.

In the lobby of the police station I apologized to TJ again. His mom was waiting to take him home. She didn't look pleased with me. My dad and Orville waited outside so I could try to make things right with TJ.

"I'm *really* sorry," I told him. "I lied to you. I used you, and I got you arrested. I haven't been much of a friend." I felt especially bad since TJ had always been so good to me.

As we were talking in the lobby, Mr. Van Andel passed by. He looked over at us but glanced away, embarrassed, when he saw it was me. I had no idea what I could do to straighten things out with TJ. And I couldn't even begin to think of how to redeem myself in Mr. Van Andel's eyes.

Mr. Van Andel went out through the front doors into the night and with him went any hope I'd ever had of winning his citizenship award. I'd *really* messed things up this time.

"It's okay, Willie," TJ told me. "No harm done. Just do me one favor."

"*Sure*," I said eagerly. "*Anything.*"

"Don't ever come near me again," TJ said.

I sighed. "Sure," I told him. "I don't know why more people don't have that policy."

The One-in-a-Million Shot

By Saturday I was still so depressed Mom let me stay home while the rest of them loaded up the car and left for Grammie's house for the birthday party. I helped Dad tie the boxes of presents on the roof rack of the car. Then I went inside and plopped down on the sofa while the rest of the family went out and piled in the car.

I lay around most of the day feeling sorry for myself. I didn't have a friend in the world. TJ never wanted to see me again—and who could blame him? Felix was up in my room working on his project. There was no way I could hang out with him. I'd been treating him like dirt for a couple of weeks now. Sam was next door at Phoebe's house, where she'd been hanging out almost every day that week, having fun without me. I was Butch without a Sundance. Or maybe I was a Sundance without a Butch.

Late that afternoon, Mom called me from Grammie's to say they'd had car trouble and wouldn't be back home till tomorrow. "Will you be okay on your own?" she asked me. She'd been very worried about me the last few days. "We'll get the car from the shop first thing in the morning and be home as soon as we can."

"Sure," I told her. "I'll be okay."

I skipped dinner, put on my pajamas, and went to bed early.

I sat up in bed suddenly. I looked over at my alarm clock. It was 2:17 in the morning. I wasn't sure what had awakened me, probably Felix talking in his sleep again—or one of the cars passing by outside. I'd fixed the window so it wouldn't stay open, but Felix had just propped it up with a book so he wouldn't suffocate. I looked over at his cot. He was breathing evenly, deeply asleep. I wanted to be his friend again.

I lay back down on the bed and stared up at the ceiling. Then I heard it.

There was a thump downstairs and then the sound of something being dragged across the floor. It sounded like someone was rearranging furniture.

I sat up in bed again, and strained to hear. Creaking. Shuffling. Footsteps. It wasn't my imagination. Someone was downstairs. Someone was in the house! *It couldn't be,* I told myself. *It couldn't be the burglar!*

I pulled back my covers and slowly slipped out of bed. If I could hear him moving around downstairs, he could hear me up here. I tiptoed over to Felix's bed. On the way I stubbed my toe. I stood there balanced on one foot, biting my hand so I wouldn't make any noise.

Downstairs the noise continued.

I stood there holding my foot with one hand—my heart pounding, my mind racing—wondering what I should do. The burglar must have seen my family pulling away in the car with all the stuff loaded on top. He must have assumed we'd all gone away for the weekend.

When the throbbing in my toe let up a little, I crept over to Felix's cot. I wasn't sure what to do. If I shook him, he might yell and let the burglar know we were in the house. I inched closer to Felix's face and, when I was close enough, I clapped my hand over his mouth. Downstairs the noises continued even louder.

Felix's eyes opened wide. He struggled and tried to yell, but the best he could manage was a frightened *urmmmm.*

"Shhhh," I hissed. "Someone's in the house. Listen."

I didn't take my hand from Felix's mouth. He stopped struggling. We were both silent a few seconds, and then there was a thumping noise downstairs followed by some creaking footsteps.

"You hear that?" I whispered.

Felix nodded. My hand still covered his mouth.

"Don't make a sound," I told him and took my hand away.

Felix sat up.

"You think it's the burglar?" he asked me.

"Yeah," I said. "I think so."

"What if it's just your folks?" he said. "Maybe they came back after all."

"Could be," I said. "But I'm not about to go down and check."

"What about the car?"

"What car?"

"If your folks are home their car will be in the driveway."

"Good idea, Buddy," I said. I crawled over Felix to the head of his cot. I pressed my face to the screen. I peered beyond the stretch of roof that ran below the bedroom windows. The dark driveway was empty, but a black pickup was parked up on the front lawn, behind the bushes. It wouldn't be visible from the street. My heart pounded. "It's *him*!" I whispered. "It's the Glenfield Burglar! It's Mr. Armed-and-Dangerous himself!"

Felix joined me at the window and looked down at the pickup. "What do we do?" he said.

"I don't know," I said. "The closest phone is in Amanda's room. He's bound to hear us if we go in there."

It was weird. We didn't talk about it—we didn't even think about it—but suddenly we were partners again. Faced with this peril, we were buddies. We were Butch and Sundance.

"Shhhh," Felix hissed. "Listen."

I held my breath and listened. What I heard made my blood run cold. It was the sound of footsteps slowly creeping up the staircase. I froze.

A dim sliver of light flickered at the crack beneath my bedroom door. He had a flashlight. The footsteps came to the top of the stairs and paused. Felix and I stared at each other in the darkness. I heard a door creak open—probably the door to my parents' bedroom.

"He's checking the bedrooms," I said. "What do we do?"

"The window," Felix whispered. He slid to the top of the cot and pushed the window screen out of its frame. It toppled and landed, with a faint clatter, on the roof outside the window.

"Shhhhhh," I told him.

"Come on," Felix said. He pulled out the book that was propping up the window. He lifted the window as far as it would go and crawled out on the roof.

Down the hall I heard more footsteps. A second door creaked open.

I scrambled to the end of Felix's cot and slipped out the window. Out on the roof I found Felix sitting with his back pressed against the wall between my window and Orville's. I scrambled across the roof tiles and joined him. As I leaned back against the wall, I heard a click. I groaned. I knew what the sound was. The window had just fallen shut and locked—exactly like I had rigged it up to do. There was no way back in the house.

"It's odd," Felix whispered. "It never *used* to do that."

This didn't seem like a good time to explain what had happened to the window.

"What are we going to do?" Felix asked.

"We've got to get help," I whispered. "We've got to get someone to call the police."

"But who?"

Just then I got an idea. "If I crawl to the other end of the roof, maybe I can get Phoebe's attention. That's one of her bedroom windows." I pointed at a small dark window on the side of Phoebe's house.

"Good idea," Felix said.

I crawled slowly across the roof. As I passed Amanda's room, a dim flashlight beam lit up her curtains from inside. I froze. A few seconds later, the curtains went dark again. I carefully crawled to the edge of the roof and looked across at Phoebe's window.

"Psssssst," I said as loudly as I dared.

I watched the window. Nothing moved.

"Psssssst," I tried again. No movement.

I looked around for something to throw at Phoebe's window. I grabbed a button from my pajamas and snapped it off.

I tossed it across the open space between the houses. It clicked against Phoebe's window and fell to the bushes below. I waited. Nothing happened.

I snapped off a second button. I threw it across a little harder. It cracked against the window. I waited. No light came on. Nothing moved.

I tore another button off. Just then Phoebe's window slid up. Sam's face looked out. Sam? What was she doing there?

"What's going on?" Sam wanted to know. She seemed a little irritated. Her blond hair was sticking up on one side of her head.

"*Shhhhhhhhh,*" I hissed, holding my finger to my lips. Wide-eyed, I pointed at my house. I held my hand up to the side of my head like I was talking on the phone.

Sam rubbed her eyes. "You want me to call your house?" she said.

"*Shhhhhhhhhhh,*" I hissed again. I pointed back at Felix. I held the phone to my ear again.

Sam shook her head. She had no idea what I was trying to tell her. "I'll be right down," she said. She slid the window shut again.

"*No, no, no!*" I whispered.

I looked back at my house. A light was moving around in Orville's room now. Felix flattened himself against the wall.

In a few seconds I heard Phoebe's door open. I heard someone tiptoe across the lawn, and then both Sam and Phoebe appeared on the other side of the bushes looking up at me.

I frantically held my fingers to my lips. "The burglar," I whispered. I pointed back at the house.

Suddenly a light came on in my room. It swept across the window. The curtains weren't drawn, so the light lit up Felix in silhouette. I scrambled up higher on the roof, next to Felix, so the burglar wouldn't see me if he looked out. The screen still lay on the roof outside my window.

Sam and Phoebe ducked down behind the bushes.

The light swept across the window again. It lit up the roof tiles and the fallen screen. Felix and I pressed our backs against the wall. I prayed hard.

"Felix," I whispered frantically. "I'm so sorry. You're still my best friend. This was all my fault. I've been a lousy friend. If we live through this, I promise I'll do my paper on the Sundance Kid. You can move everything you want into the room. You can even keep the window—"

"He's at the window," Sam called up to us in a whisper. I held my breath and pushed my back against the wall. Out of the corner of my eye, I could see a shadowy figure in the window just a few inches away.

My mind raced. I prayed that God would help me find a way out of this. I had to come up with an idea—and then it hit me. It was a million-to-one shot, but it just might work.

"The doorbell," I called down softly. "Throw a rock. He'll think someone's at the door. Maybe he'll run out the back door."

Sam looked over the bushes at the front door, which I couldn't see. I knew the doorbell was less than an inch in diameter, and Sam must have been about 30 yards away.

She shook her head. "It can't be done," she whispered.

I heard the sound of someone fiddling with the window latch beside me. I could see black-gloved fingers trying to unlock it.

"The girl who knocked over all three milk bottles can do it," I told her, trying to encourage her. "You've got to try."

"Okay," a voice piped up—*but it wasn't Sam.*

Phoebe leaped up from behind the bushes with a huge rock in one hand. She went into that weird windup of hers. My mouth dropped open. Her arm spun like a propeller.

I held my hands up in front of me. *"No, not—"*

But before anyone could stop her, Phoebe flung the big stone in the general direction of the house.

It truly *was* a one-in-a-million shot. She was aiming at the doorbell, but the rock flew up toward me in the moonlight.

I flung myself down on the roof and heard a splash of glass behind me. I squeezed my eyes shut. I prayed at the speed of light.

I lay praying, my heart pounding. Someone tapped me on the shoulder.

"Dude, you've got to see this," Felix said. He was looking in the shattered bedroom window. I scrambled up beside him.

There, stretched out on Felix's cot amid all the broken glass, was a man dressed in black. Phoebe had knocked the burglar cold.

We called 911, and the man was still unconscious when Sam led the police and the paramedics up to my room.

Phoebe, of course, insisted that she had actually been *aiming* at the burglar—but I knew for a fact she wasn't even looking in that direction when she threw the stone.

⑫

Lesson Learned

A few days later Sam, Phoebe, and I were in the kitchen drinking sodas when the doorbell rang. It was Felix.

"Come on in, Buddy," I told him. "Everybody's here. Let me get you a soda." Felix followed me to the kitchen. We were friends again. His parents had come back, and we were no longer roommates.

In fact, I had learned a lot about Felix and me. Instead of being his friend, I had turned him into my enemy. I hadn't followed Jesus' words in Luke 10 at all.

After we helped catch the Glenfield burglar, I read the story of the Good Samaritan again. I had been so focused on being a good neighbor to win an award, I'd missed the point entirely—Jesus was saying we are to love even our enemies perfectly. I sure hadn't done that—I *can't* do that. Only Jesus can. I asked God to forgive me for the way I'd

treated Felix and the way I'd been acting lately. I
know God forgave me and Felix forgave me too.

Now everything seemed back to normal. My
room no longer looked like a warehouse. Orville's
girlfriend was talking to him again. The Glenfield Burglar was behind bars. I just wished there were something I could do for TJ. He was the one who ended up
with the short end of the stick.

When Felix and I got to the kitchen, I noticed he
had a newspaper with him. "You don't have to pick up
the paper anymore," I told him. "Your parents are
back, and the burglar is out of commission."

He glanced down at the paper. "I know," he said.
"I just brought it to see if there were any more articles
about us helping catch the guy."

"Let *me* look," Phoebe squealed excitedly. She
jumped up from the table, grabbed the paper, and flattened it out on the kitchen counter. The rest of us
grinned. Phoebe had emerged as quite a hero, always
insisting that she'd actually intended to knock the
burglar cold. She'd been collecting newspaper clip-
pings about her daring deed for her scrapbook.

I opened the refrigerator, handed Felix a soda,
and sat down at the table again. "When you're done
with that newspaper, can I look at it?" I asked Phoebe.
She nodded without looking up.

"You're not still looking for volunteer jobs are
you?" Felix asked me. He took Phoebe's seat at the

table. "I thought you'd given up on the Van Andel Award."

I laughed. "Yeah," I said. "I've given up on the award. But I thought I might just do some volunteer work on my own. Just to help out."

"Sounds like you learned something from all this," Sam said.

"Yeah," I said. "I learned that your neighbors aren't just the people who live next door to you."

"You think you could find something we could do together?" Felix asked. He popped open his can of soda. "We could be like Butch and Sundance again— except doing good stuff instead of robbing banks."

"How about Butch, Sundance, *and* Annie Oakley?" Sam chimed in. "I'd like to do it too."

"Sure," I said. "Maybe we can find something if we ever get the newspaper away from Phoebe."

Phoebe folded the newspaper backwards and brought it over to the table. She put it down in front of me. "There's something in here you should see," Phoebe said.

"A good volunteer job?" I asked her.

"Not exactly," she said. She flattened out the paper and pointed at a small article on the second page.

Local Boy Wins Van Andel Award

Thomas Jefferson Drew, who goes by TJ, was awarded this year's Van Andel Citizenship Award. A computer purchase grant of $10,000 will be awarded to Glenfield High School, where Drew is a sophomore, in recognition of his outstanding community service.

"He's an example to all of us," Stephen Van Andel, donor of the award, said. "It seems like I've seen this fine young man all over town, working hard to make Glenfield a better place. I was most impressed when I saw him at the county jail, counseling a juvenile delinquent."

I laughed out loud. "*I* was that juvenile delinquent," I told them. "I guess I helped TJ out after all."

① iNVASiON from planet X
the misadventures of Willie Plummet

② submarine SaNDWiCHeD
the misadventures of Willie Plummet

③ ANYtHiNG you can do I can do BeTTeR
Willie Plummet

⑦ TidaL WaVe
Willie Plummet

⑧ Shooting stARs
the misadventures of Willie Plummet

⑨ HaiL to the CHUMP
the misadventures of Willie Plummet

⑬ stuck on you
the misadventures of Willie Plummet

⑭ dOg days
the misadventures of Willie Plummet

⑮ BRaiN FREEzE
the misadventures of Willie Plummet